A mysterioı soul brought forth from the Ancient Americas forced to deal with negative karma placed on by The Creators for abusing it's freewill. Upon doing so sparked a effect by banishing it to the low earthly realms, Isolated from the world and giving It the only chance to clear all 3.D. debt by unleashing 12 phases of creation using its given weapon, The Power Pen.

HELLO READER, IT SEEMS THE CREATORS BROUGHT YOU TO THE RIGHT BOOK, IN DIVINE TIME
THE FIRST PHASE OF CREATION
STARTS IN 3..2...1

DIMENSIONAL KEY

BRUSH!
BRUSH

TABLE OF CONTENTS

CHAPTER 1-HALF-DAY 1

CHAPTER 2-SHORT-CUT 18

CHAPTER 3-BORING LECTURE..............36

CHAPTER 4-OFF LIMITS................................52

CHAPTER 5-BLUE BASEBALL....................70

CHAPTER6-DON'T TOUCH IT....................86

CHAPTER 7-SUMMER BEGINS..................103

CHAPTER 8-SET THE ENGINES..................118

CHAPTER 9-GOOD-BYE................................133

CHAPTER 10-WHAT'S MY PURPOSE..........151

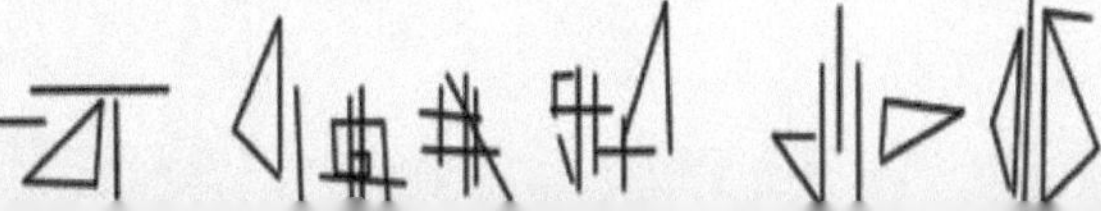

CHAPTER
1
HALF DAY
YA-
WN

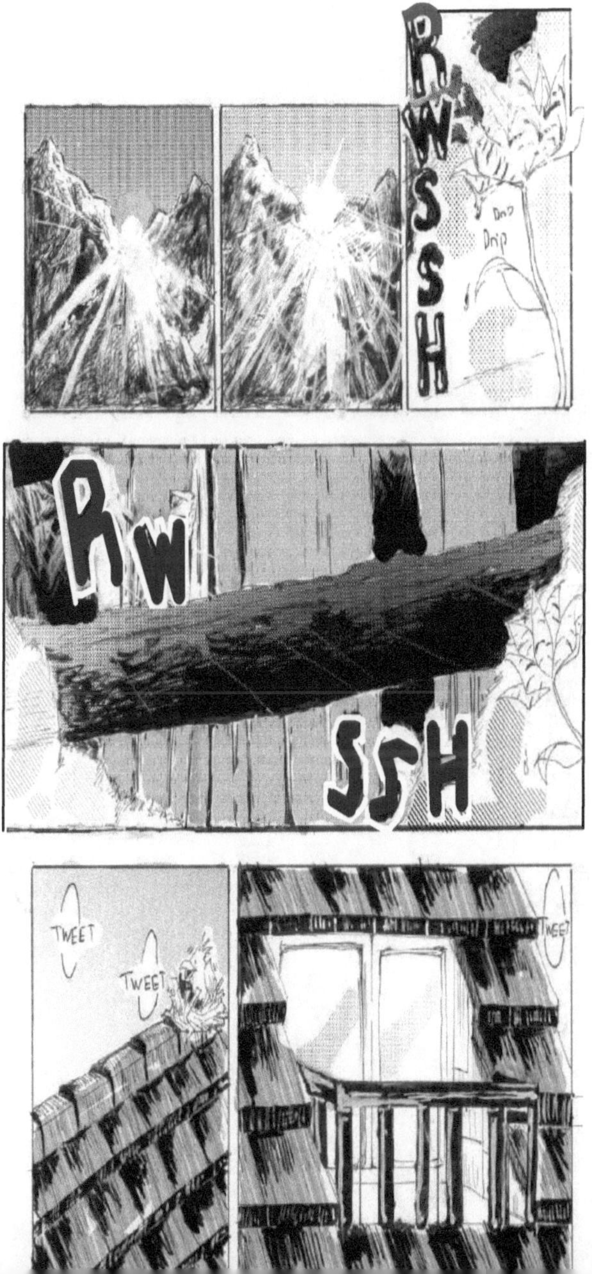

RWSSH
Drip
Drip
RW
SSH
TWEET
TWEET

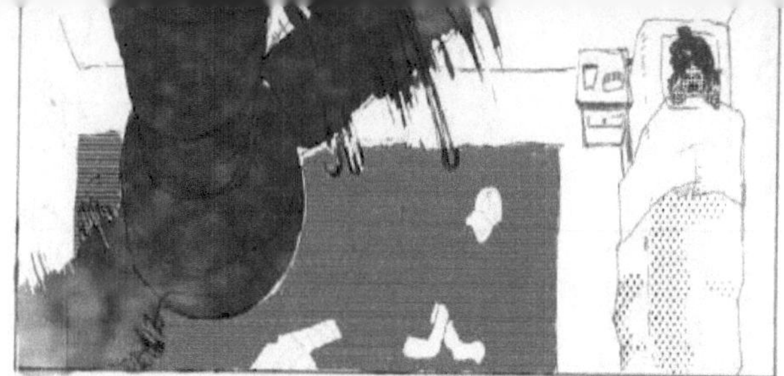

Tick
SNORE

PEI, DEAR WAKE UP ITS PAST ELEVEN O'CLOCK
BA NG!!
HURRY OR YOU'LL BE LATE FOR SCHOOL!!!

UH!?
AAHHH

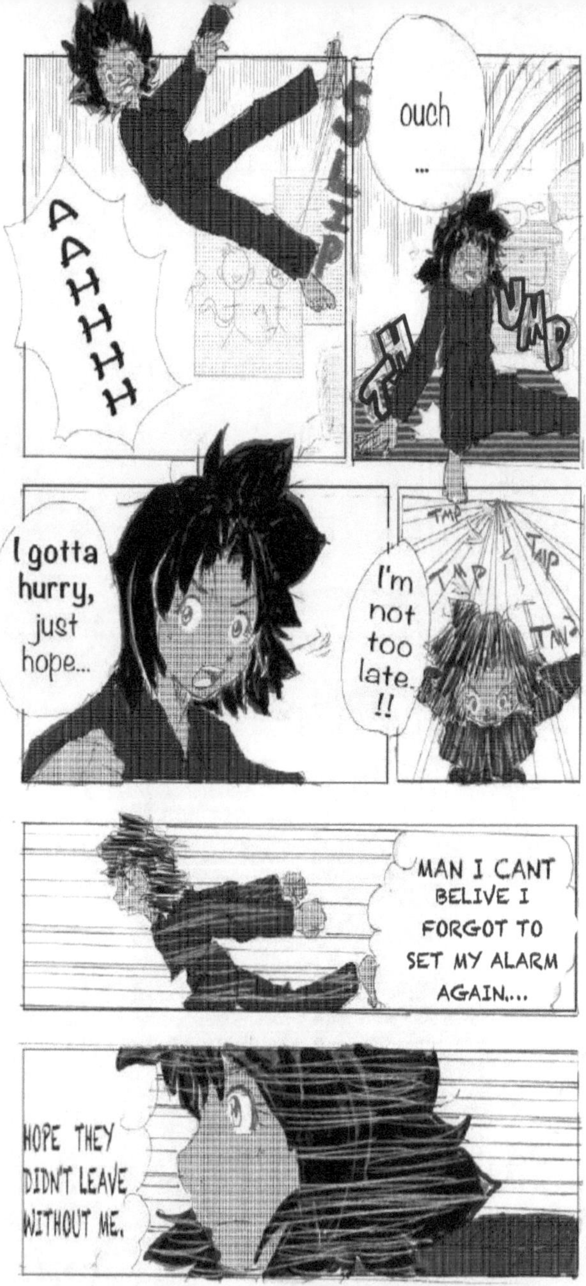

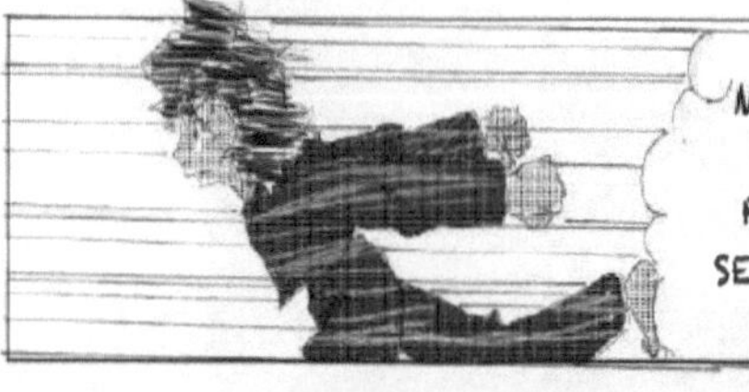

ouch
...
AAHHH
I gotta hurry, just hope...
I'm not too late.!!
TMP
TMP
TMP
TMP

MAN I CANT BELIVE I FORGOT TO SET MY ALARM AGAIN....
HOPE THEY DIDN'T LEAVE WITHOUT ME.

FSSSH
SQUIRT
Brush Brush
MAN... I OVER SLEPT AGAIN. BUT...
THAT DREAM.... IT WAS SO REAL.
CHEW
POUR

KRABLE POP
KRACKLE POP
FSHT FSHT

I SEE SOME-ONE FORGOT TO
FSH 7

SET THIER ALARM THIS MORNING.

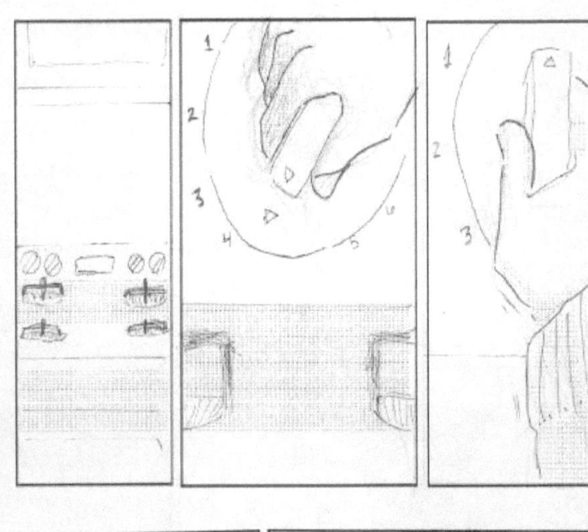

NEWS 11
RING

RING
RING
WHO COULD BE CALLING THIS EARLY ???

OH NO....
I HOPE ITS NOT THE DEBT COLLECTORS !!!!
RING
BA DUM
BA DUM

THIS IS THE FA HOUSE
MRS FA ITS SHEN...
OH HELLO DEAR ARE YOU CALLING FOR PEL...
GRAB

SWEETIE SHEN JUST CALLED AND SAID HE WANTS YOU YO HURRY.
DIM
DIM
DIM
Tmp
Tmp

DIM
SS CRR REEECH

!
HE BETTER NOT LEAVE WITH OUT ME.

AREN'T YOU FORGETTING SOMETHING IMPORTANT?

UH?...
GRANDPA WHAT ARE
YOU TALKING ABOUT?

YOUR SCHOOL CLOTHES !!!!....

Eh?
...
OOPS
.....
ZOOOM!!
BE RIGHT BACK!!!
PULL
TUG
STRETCH

TA-DA ... AND DONE.
TH-RUF
SEE YA LATER MOM ...
Wave!
LOVE YOU ...
BEFORE YOU GO MAKE SURE . YOU CLEAN YOUR PLATE.
BYE
NO TIME GRAND-MA, GOTTA ... HURRY
TMP
TMP
TMP

IT'S ALMOST TIME ...
SHE'LL BE HERE ANY MINUTE NOW...
GULP I HOPE ...
VROOOONNN!!
... READY TO GO RAJ.
TAP TAP

TMP
TMP
GChOOM
STARE
TMP
TMP
THE COUNT-DOWN BEGINS IN ... THREE
... TWO. ... ONE
WOOOOOOO

SHOO
GROWL

SsSHHHOOOMMM

SHOO...
FSH
SHOO

SSHHHOOOOMMM
THUNDER
THUNDER
ON TO GET THE OTHERS !!!!

CHAPTER 2

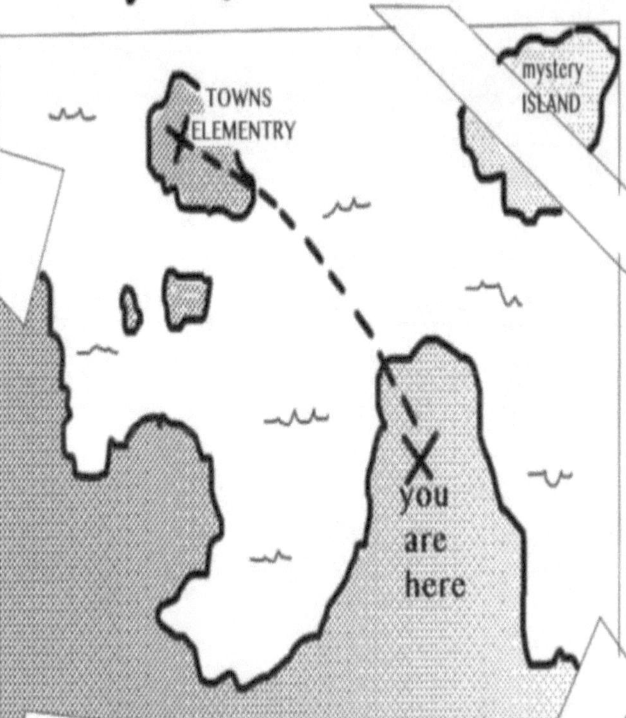

SHORT CUT

PACKIN' THIS NOW SURE SAVES TIME FOR LATER.
FSSHH

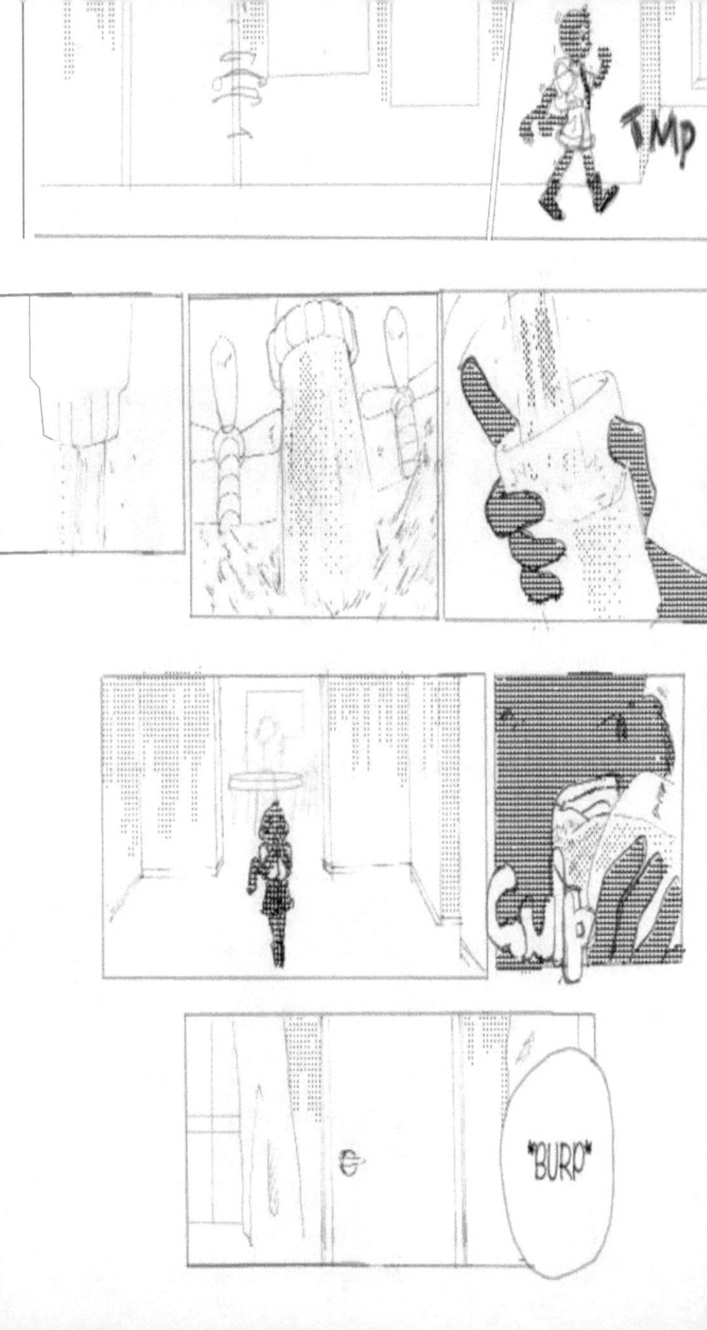
TMP
Gulp
Gulp
BURP

YOUNG
MAN
...
FLINCH
UH

UMM
I

PLEASE
DON'T TELL ME
A GLASS OF
WATER
AND AN
APPLE
IS ALL THAT
YOUR EATING.
FOR
BREAKFAST
THIS
MORNING
SIR.

B-BUT I ATE SOMTHING THIS TIME ...
HONESTLY. MOM
YOU NEED TO EAT

I DONT BUY FOOD EVERY MONTH FOR IT TO GO TO WASTE
IF YOU THINK EATING AN APPLE IS GOING TO -

DONT SWEAT IT SON, WHEN I WAS YOUR AGE WE USED SAY AN APPLE
A DAY KEEPS THE DOCTOR AWAY.
YOUR REALLY NOT HELPING DEAR !

YOUR OVER-REACTING ... ITS ONLY A HALF OF A DAY OF SHOOL
HE'LL BE BACK LATER AND HE CAN EAT ALL THE FOOD HE-

GROCERIES AROUND HERE,
IF IM GOIING TO BE THE ONE BUYING ...
WELL BE EATING ON MY CHOICE OF DIET AND-

GRAB
DONT YOU LEAVE JUST YET SIR !!!!
ALMOST THRERE
LOVE YOU ... BYE MOM.

SHUT
"SIGH"
THE THINGS
I GET FOR
BEING A
CARING
MOTHER
...

AND A EASY
COMPATABLE
WIFE, WHY
IS IT JUST
SO
...
HARD
ASKING
EVERY-
ONE
TO
EAT A
HEALTHY
BALANCED
DIET
EVERY DAY
...
I JUST DONT
GET IT.
NEW

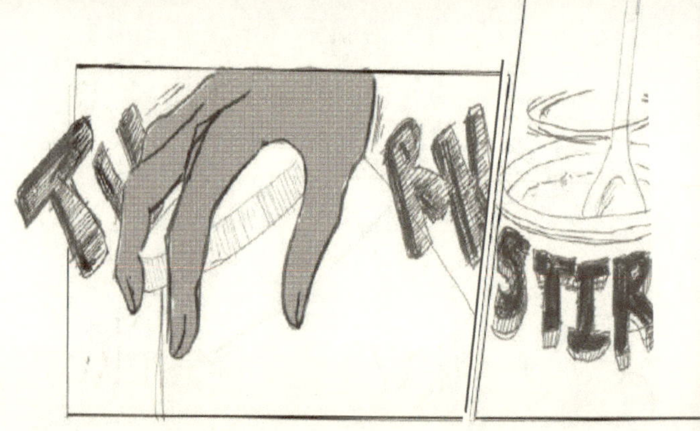
TIC TAC STIR

SO WHAT WERE YOU SAYING ABOUT OUR GROCEY BUDJET...
MEW
UM NOTHING NEVERMIND ERR... JUST FORGET IT.

HEY PEI
YOU MADE
IT,

FINALLY.

THERE NO TIME,
WE HAVE TO
HURRY BEFORE SHEN
GOES ON HIS OWN...
YOU KNOW HOW
HE IS WITH HIS
FUTURE STUDIES.

RELAX
...
YOU KNOW HE'S WEIRD ABOUT STUFF
LIKE THAT.

DOESN'T HE KNOW THAT STUFF IS DONE IN AND DURING SCHOOL
...
AND NOT IN THE SUMMER?

PEDAL
HUFF
SPARKLE
HUFF

HUFF
HUFF
HUFF
GOTTA HURRY... GOTTA GO FASTER. !!!!!!......
SHOO
VOOMM

Huff
Huff
Huff
pedal
pedal
I SHOULD'VE WAITED BUT I COULDN'T MISS THIS LAST DAY OF SCHOOL, ITS JUST TOO IMPORTANT

PEDAL
slick
PEDAL
PEDAL
POP
O!

MY BREAKS ARE OUT !!!!!
SCREEEETCH

SK*r*h
GASP
*SCREECH
AAHHH!!
SHOOOM

AAAAAAAAHHHHHHHHHH!!
THUD

AM ...
I..DEAD

WHAT IS THAT...
IS THAT AN ANGEL?

SHEN!!!!
TMP

HOLD ON BUDDY!!!
TMP
TMP
TMP
TMP
YEA

YOU ALL RIGHT?
YOU KNOW...
YOU REALLY HAVE TO—
STOP DOING STUFF ON YOUR OWN.

WE WON'T MAKE IT.
IF WE WAIST ANY MORE TIME.
IM GOOD
NOW LETS GO
AND NO ONE IS GOING TO STOP ME !!!!
I AM GOING TO GET TO SCHOOL ON TIME ...
SOME-TIMES YOU...
REALLY SCARE ME.
ARE SURE YOU DONT NEED THE NURSE FIRST?

FLUTER
WOO OO OO
ITS ALMOST TIME, HEY PEI IS THERE ANY
WAY YOU COULD FLY FASTER?
IF I DO WE ALL...
MIGHT FALL OFF

95
DUDE, YOU REALY ARE GETTING CRAZY
AREN'T YOU?
WOOOO
SIGH I JUST WANT TO GET TO SCHOOL ON TIME.
SIGN
I HAVE A FASTER WAY,
A SHORT CUT.

CHAPTER 3

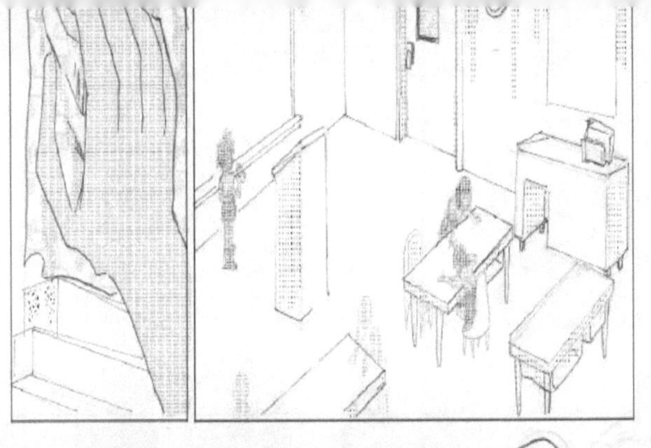

PLEASE EVERY-ONE GET TO YOUR SEATS
CLASS WILL BE STARTING SOON

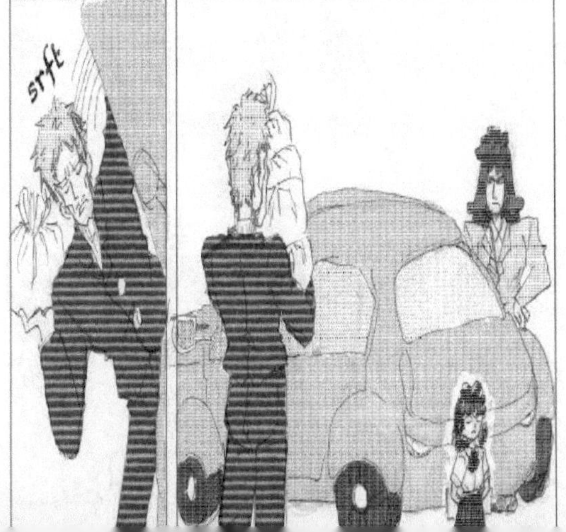
srft

HEY COME ON..
HURRY MARYON.
SO?
DID YOU BRING THE STUFF?
FFFSSHHH
EVEN SOMTHING BETTER.. YOU KNOW ME,
ALWAYS SETTING THE BAR HIGH...
TUSSLE TUSSLE!
BEING CLASS PRESIDENT AINT EASY.
OH LOOK IT'S THE TWO LOSERS
AND OF COURSE THEY BROUGHT THAT..
YELLOW EYED GOGGLED WEIRDO.
ISN'T HER FAMILY CRIMINALS OR SOMTHING ???

GREAT SHES GOING TO RUIN IT LIKE LAST TIME, SHE SHOULD'VE STAYED HOME
OR SOME-THING.
FLUTTER
IT'S ALMOST TIME....
EVERY-ONE IN MY GROUP...
REPORT FOR....
CLASS A GRADE 5 OVER HERE.

IM GLAD YOU ALL MADE IT. AS YOU KNOW...
TODAY IS SPECIAL FOR OUR STUDIES DUE TO LAST YEAR'S INTERUPTIONS

I'LL EXPLAIN MORE IN THE CLASSROOM.

CHATTER
CHATTER
BLAH
CHILDREN QUIET DOWN...
BLAH
BLAH

dream board
AND EVERYONE TO YOUR SEATS... QUICKLY.
3
BLAH
BLAH

HOW IS EVERYONE, CAUSE IM GLAD YOU ALL MADE IT THIS MORING
NOW BEFORE THE COMING ANOUCEMENT FIRST I WOULD LIKE TO ...
THANK THE TEACHER'S FACULTY STAFF
AND CHAPERONES FOR TODAY.
ITS AN HOUNER FOR ALLOWING ...
OUR STUDIES TO EXPAND
INTO THINGS GREATER.
LUCKLY FOR US WE GOT VALIDATION
IN OUR STUDIES TO MAKE
UP, DUE TO BAD WEATHER THIS WINTER

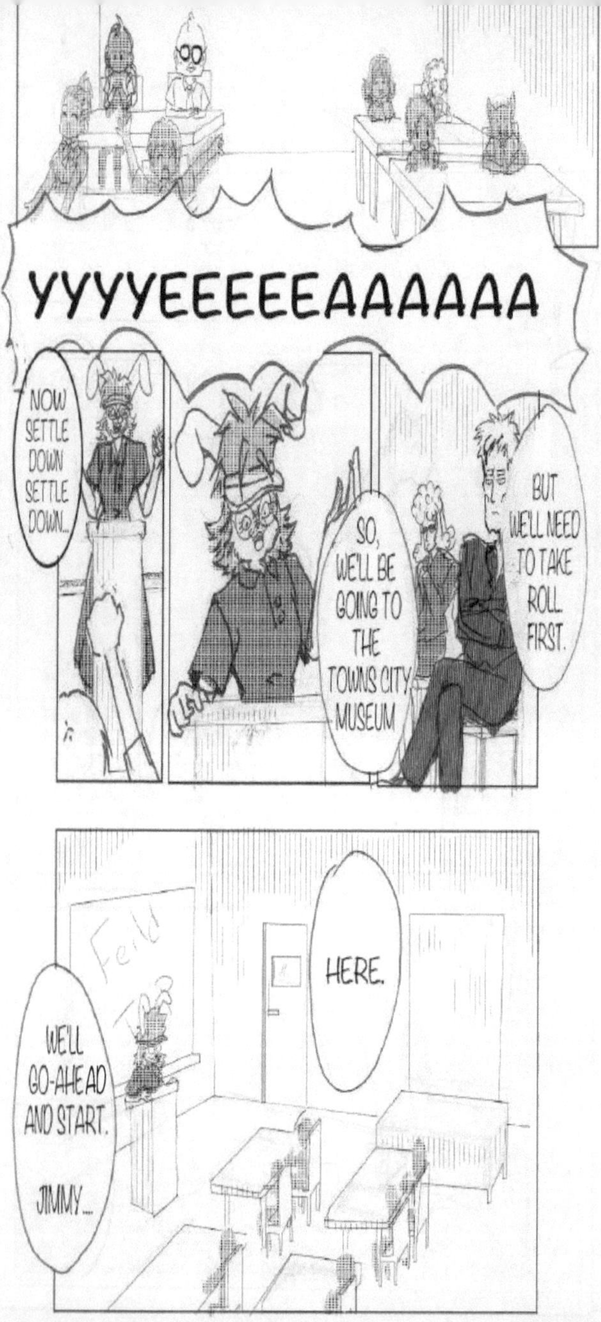

YYYYEEEEEAAAAAA
NOW SETTLE DOWN SETTLE DOWN...
SO, WE'LL BE GOING TO THE TOWNS CITY MUSEUM
BUT WE'LL NEED TO TAKE ROLL FIRST.
WE'LL GO-AHEAD AND START.
JIMMY...
HERE.

SHAWN
...
HERE
WOW, SHE
EVEN MORE
ALURING
UP-CLOSE
...

ER ...I
MEAN
HI

OH NO
MY BOOK,
I BETTER
PUT...
IT AWAY
BEFORE
SHE SEES
IT
!!!

"GAH"

AAAHHH

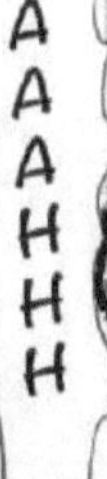

THUMP

AW MAN,
THERE
GOES MY
CHANCE
!!!

TERRIN

IM
WAVE
HERE

HERE
SHEN

POW

. . .

POW
HERE

SUSIE...
AND TARA.
IS ALL ACOUNTED FOR ROLL HERE
CLASS...
YES !!!
CLASS, GET IN A SINGLE FILE LINE PLEASE.

Types of Clouds
CHATTER
CHATTER

SSHH, QUIET DOWN...
THE HALLS

WHEN WE GET TO THE BUS I WANT ALL TO BE ON YOUR
BEST BEHAVIOR...

OUR DRIVER NEEDS...
TO GET US THERE
SAFELY, SO KEEP THE NOISE LOW.

FWISH
WELL... HOWDY KIDDOS.

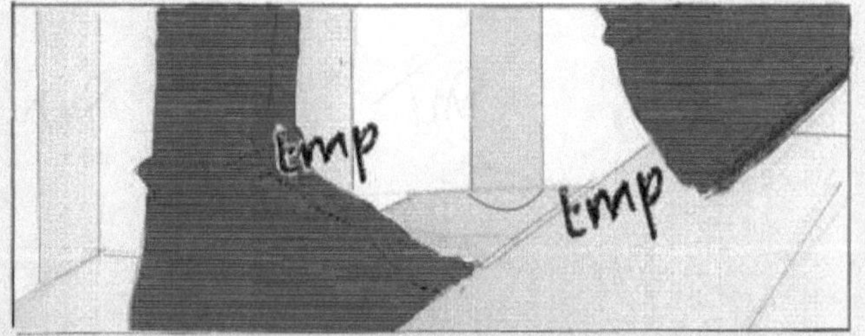

tmp
tmp

LETS MAKE SURE
ALL IS ATTENTED FOR

ONE, TWO ....
THREE, FOUR ....
FIVE ....
SIX ....

VOOM

VRRRRNNNNN

READY FOR THIS AWSOME

FEILDTRIP PEI

THE ONLY THING SHE NEEDS... IS TO GO BACK TO IS THE FREAK-SHOW.

LAUGHS

ONLY VALUABLE PEOPLE EXIST HERE

AND YOU TWO ARENT.

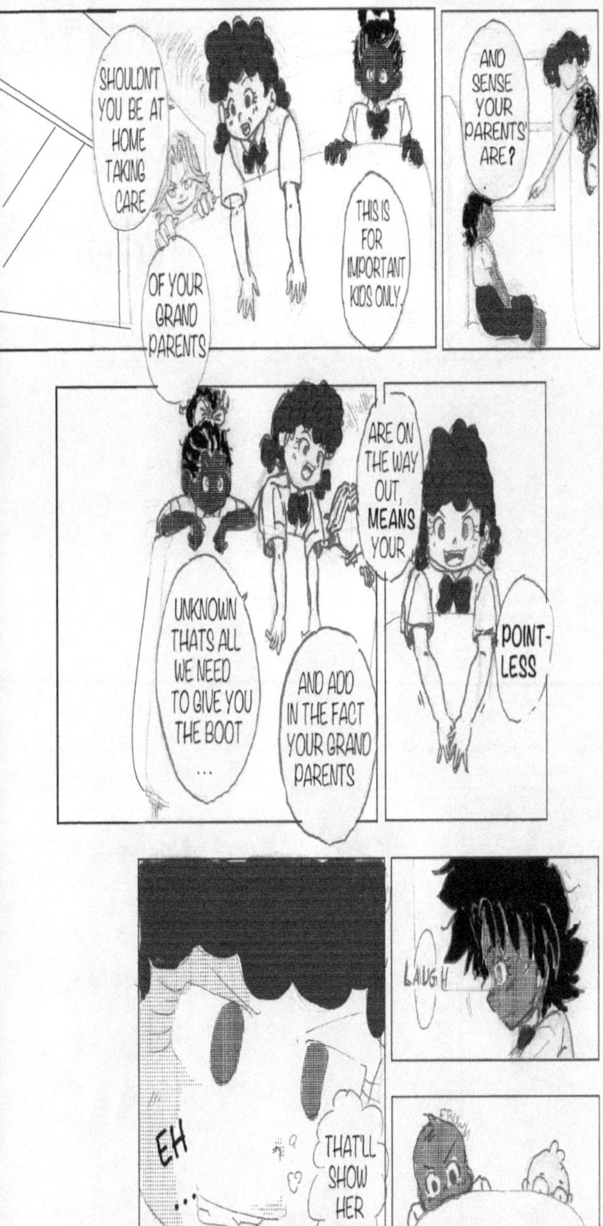

SHOULDN'T YOU BE AT HOME TAKING CARE
OF YOUR GRAND PARENTS
THIS IS FOR IMPORTANT KIDS ONLY
AND SENSE YOUR PARENTS' ARE?
ARE ON THE WAY OUT, MEANS YOUR
UNKNOWN THATS ALL WE NEED TO GIVE YOU THE BOOT ...
AND ADD IN THE FACT YOUR GRAND PARENTS
POINT-LESS
LAUGH
EH ...
THAT'LL SHOW HER ...
FROWN

BLAH
BLAH
BLAH
BLAH
OH SHUT UP MARYON !!!!

YOUR JUST JEALOUS CAUSE PEI'S FAMILY IS
ALOT MORE COOLER THAN YOURS.

AT LEAST SHE GETS THE TIME...
AND ATTENTION YOU NEVER WILL.
GRRR Bh

WHY YOU
LITTLE
IMP
...
WHO
DO YOU
THINK
YOU ARE
!!!!

HEY GUYS,
LOOK
...

WERE
HERE.
TOWN CITY
MUSEUM
OF HISTORY

WHEN WE GET OFF THE BUS
I WANT EVERYONE IN A SINGLE FILE...
SHUUN

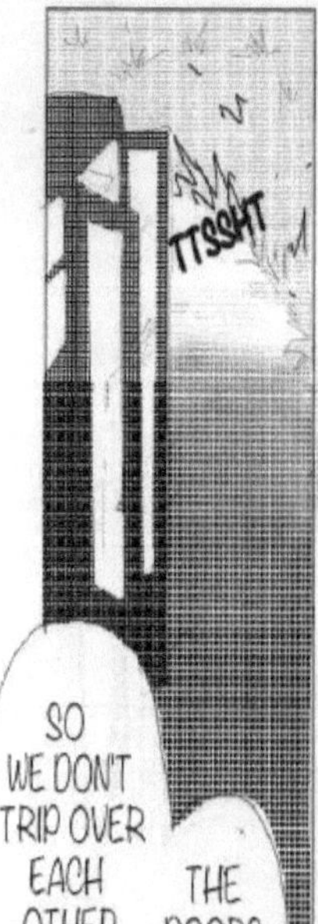

TTSSHT
SO WE DON'T TRIP OVER EACH OTHER AS
THE DOORS OPEN.

WELL SHALL BEGIN...

CHAPTER 4

OFF LIMITS

HELLO STUDENTS, WELCOME TO OUR BELOVED MUSEM
ONE OF THE LARGEST IN THE STATE,
FILLED WITH MUCH KNOWLEDGE TO BE ABSORBED

NOW BEFORE WE CONTINUE, CAN ANYONE TELL ME
SOME FACTS ABOUT OUR MUSEM

YOU YOUNGMAN IN THE FRONT

THIS BUILDING WAS FOUND IN 1809 BY CHARLES S BALDAMIR ...
IS THE FIRST OF OUR SCIENTIST IN OUR NATION

ANYONE HAVE ANY FURTHER FACTS
OR QUESTIONS TO ADD?
NO !!!
BATH-- ROOMS ON YOUR RIGHT
AND REC HALL IS ON YOUR LEFT
NOW LETS BEGIN OUR TOUR.
HOUR PAST
COME BOYS AND GIRLS JUST A BIT HIKE MORE

AND WERE HERE ...
COME ON, JUST A COUPLE MORE STRIDES
TMP
TMP
HUFF
HUFF
HUFF

NOW HOLD IT !!!

BEFORE WE PROCEED THERE IS ONE RULE WE MUST FOLLOW UNDERSTAND

AND THAT IS ...
STAY TOGETHER AT ALL TIMES.

NOW, WE SHALL BEGIN WITH OUR FISRT SITE.
THIS ROCK CARBON DATED TO THE ONLY FRAGMENT OF AN...
ASTROIED ABOUT 3 BILLION YEARS AGO.
Site I

IN THE BEGINNING OUR PLANET WAS BIRTHED FROM A COLLISION...
BO

WITH THE TWO CONSTRUCTING THROUGH DEBREE TAKING THOUNSANDS OF YEARS TO FORM.
KR
RSK

THUS OUR BLUE PLANET WAS BORN
AND LIFE WAS FORMED, FROM PLANTS...

TO GREAT GEOLOGICAL FEATURES...

TO SENTIENT CREATURES.

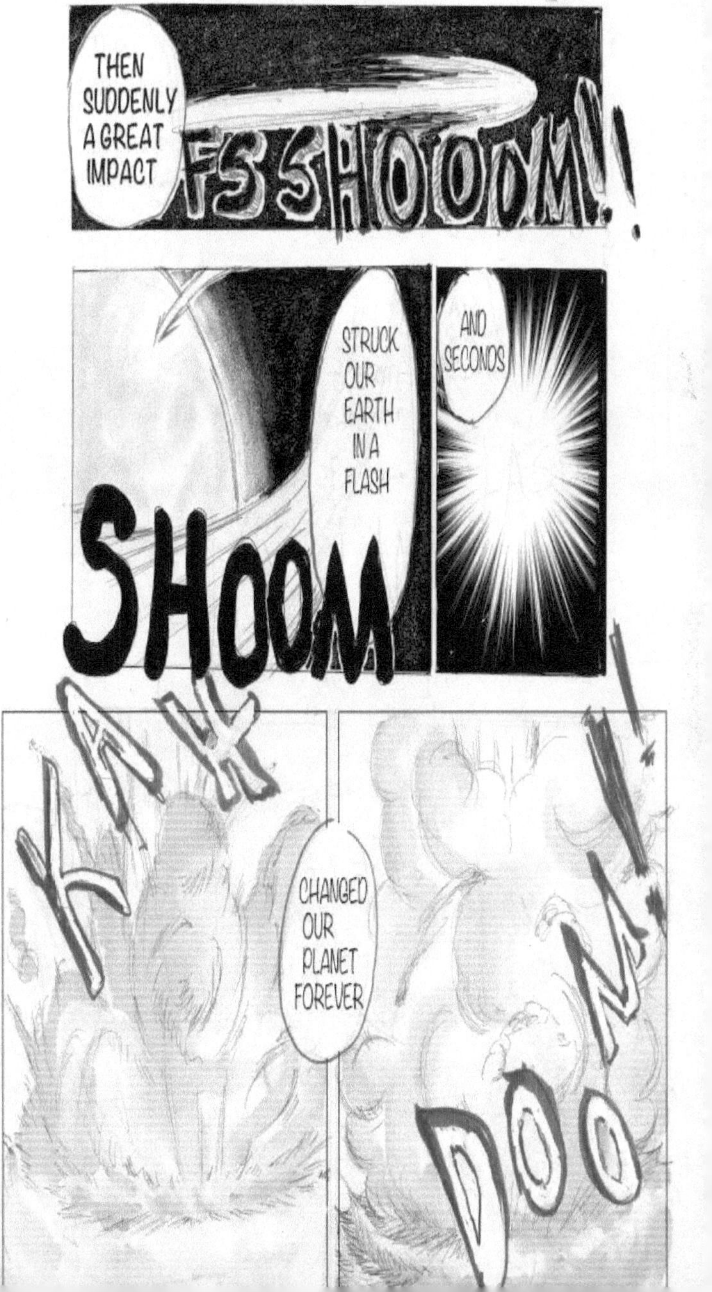

THEN SUDDENLY A GREAT IMPACT
FSSHOOOM!!
SHOOM
STRUCK OUR EARTH IN A FLASH
CHANGED OUR PLANET FOREVER

AND SECONDS

KA-
TOOH
KILLING 75% OF LIFE ON EARTH.
BUT IN SHORT, A NEW PHASE STARTED.
GRAB
...THE AGE OF MAMMALS
BUT NOT ALL LIFE PERISHED UNLUCKILY.
SOME KINGDOMS ADOPTED TO HARSH CONDITIONS
NOTABLY THE BLUE AND GREEN FUNGI.

BUT THE IMPACT MAKING FOOD SCARCE...

THE BEINGS HAD TO ADAPT TO THE ABUNDANT FUNGI
Sniff Sniff
AND WITH JUST ONE BITE CAUSED A GREAT

MUTATION IN THE BODY
BEGINING TO EXPAND INTO A

HUMANOID LOOK, FEEL AND APPERANCE.

PHYSICAL TRAITS WASN'T THE ONLY CHANGE,
INTELLECT RAPIDLY INCREASED.

ALLOWING VERBAL SPEACH AND
CULTRAL LANGUAGE, CUSTOMS AND BEHAVIOR.

ONE OF THE MAJOR TRAITS OF THE KUFA WAS THIER SIMPLISTIC DESIGN.

BLENDING ALL OF THIS, CREATES THE VERY FABRIC OF OUR SPECIES.
SITE 1

ANYONE HAVE ANY QUESTIONS BEFORE WE WRAP UP THIS AREA?
WHAT ABOUT THOSE CAVES OVER THERE?

THESE CAVES USED TO BE PART OF OUR TOUR...
BUT DUE TO THE UNSTABLE STRUCTURE, WE NO LONGER ALLOW THIS ANYMORE.

SO...
THE CAVES
ARE COMPLETELY
OFF LIMITS...
UNDERSTAND.
YES

NOW THEN,
WE'LL MOVE
ON TO OUR
SECOND SITE,
THE KUFA'S
CULTURE

AND
THIER
WAYS OF
LIVING.

OH GREAT...
HERE COMES
ANOTHER
BORING
LECTRUE...
WHEN
ARE
WE GONNA
GET TO
THE FUN
STUFF?

!
SHSHH
I CANT HEAR

ROLLS EYES
SIGH

HEY PEI, DO YOU WANNA DITCH THIS LECTRUE
AND LET THE REAL EXPLORING BEGIN?
whisper

EXPLORING !?

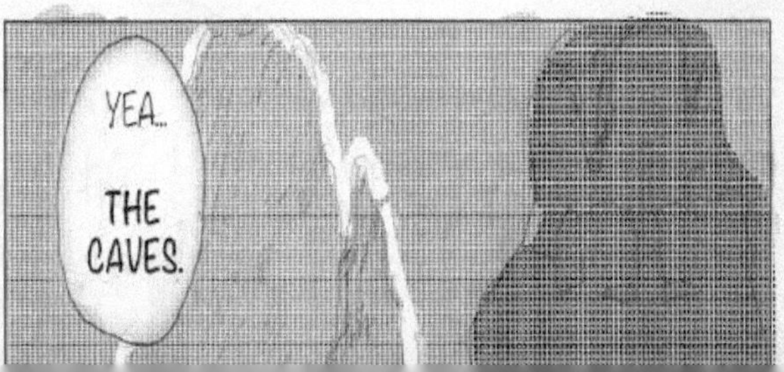
YEA..
THE CAVES.

HHHMMM...
THOSE CAVES DO SOUND INTRESTING

TMP
TMP
TMP
TMP

TMP
TMP
MAN THIS TOUR IS PRETTY AWSOM--

UH... GUYS?

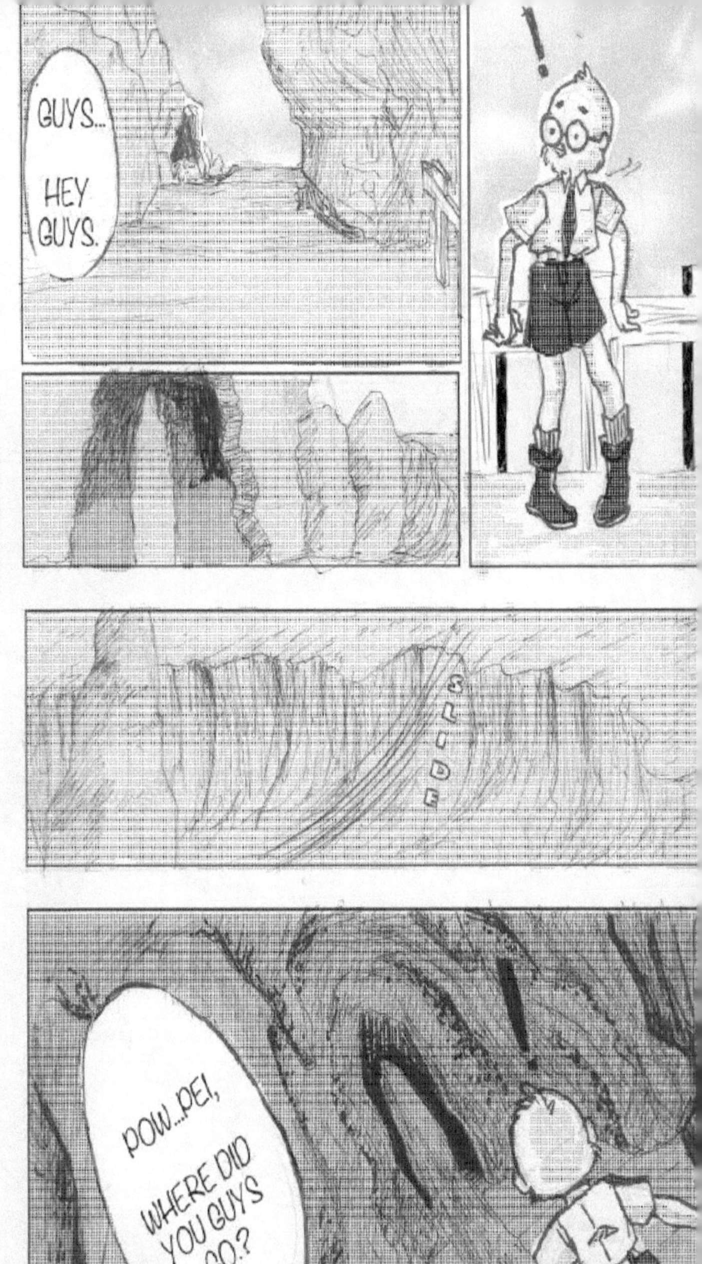

GUYS...
HEY GUYS.
SLIDE
POW...PEI,
WHERE DID YOU GUYS GO.?

HELLO !!!

GULP
GUYS ...
EBELAHLAHLA AHAHLHAHAH AHAHHAAHHA !!!!!!

AAAA
HHHH
!!!!

WHY'D YOU DO THAT FOR, BESIDES . . .
WE'RE NOT SUPPOSED TO BE HERE
AND WHERE'S PEI!?
HEY GUYS,

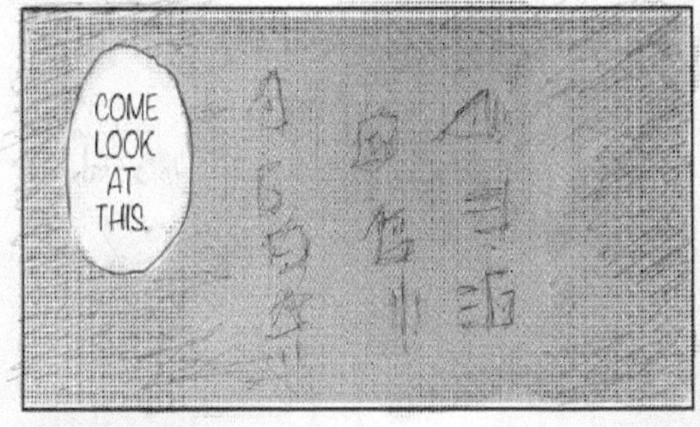

COME LOOK AT THIS.

WOW ITS LOOKS COOL, LIKE A BUCH ART ...
DRAWINGS AND STUFF.

HEY ...
THERE'S MORE ...

MAN, HOW DEEP DOES THIS CAVE GO!?

SHEN, YOU SHOULD GET SOME PICTRUES
AND ADD IT TO YOUR SCRAP COLLECTION.

IT IS COOL,
BUT I THINK ITS BETTER
IF WE GO BACK.
DON'T CHA WANNA GET AHEAD OF YOUR STUDIES FOR NEXT YEAR?

OH COME ON THIS IS BETTER THAN ANY GUIDE COULD OFFER
NO MATTER HOW COOL IT IS.
IM NOT GETTING IN TROUBLE

THEN I GUESS YOU HAVE TO STAY HERE
IN THE DARK SHADOWY DEPTHS
OF THE CAVES
. . .

CHAPTER 5

BLUE BASEBALL

ALONE...
RIGHT PEI...

PEI?

STARE

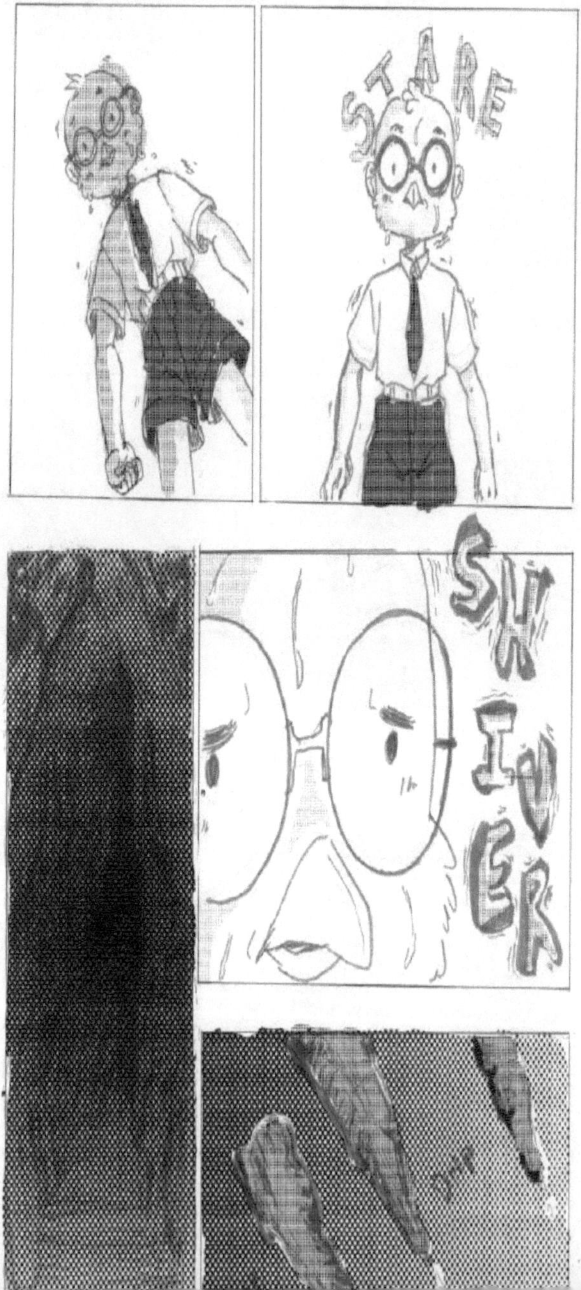

STARE

SHIVER

WOOOOO OOOOOO
WOOOOOO

BA-DUM
BA-DUM
BADUM
GULP
WAIT
FOR
ME
!!!

SHO OOM

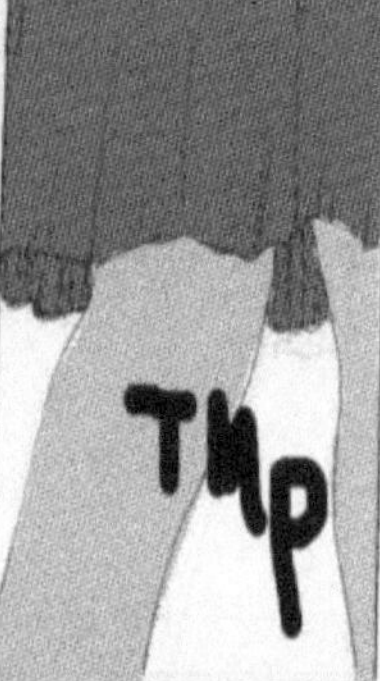

HEY

CAN YOU MAKE IT A BIT LIGHTER ...
ITS GETTIN' HARD TO SEE.

MH!
... I JUST CHANGED THIS THING.

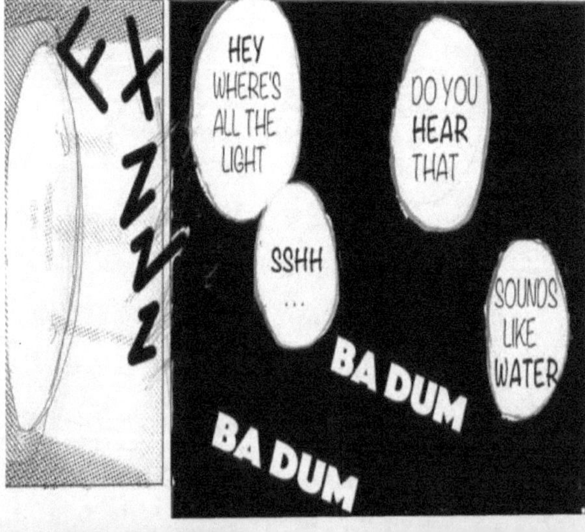

HEY WHERE'S ALL THE LIGHT
SSHH ...
DO YOU HEAR THAT
SOUNDS LIKE WATER
BA DUM
BA DUM

AND FOOT STEPS...
ITS GETTING CLOSER.

I THOUGHT YOU GUYS NEEDED A LITTLE LIGHT,

EH!?
EH!?

LOOK, IF YOU GET IN TROUBLE, WE ALL GET IN TROUBLE
...
BESIDES I WOULD FEEL GUILTY THAT I SAW YOU AND DIDN'T SAY ANYTHING.

AND SO, I DECIED TO TAKE ...
ONE FOR THE TEAM
WOW .... I'M SUPRISED.
YEA, SO BRAVE.

OH AND ANOTHER THING. WAS ...

I'M ALSO AFRAID OF THE DARK.

WELL, NOW THAT WE KNOW
WHO'S FEET THOSE ARE.
TO FIND WHERE THAT WATER IS COMING FROM
OH, RIGHT ...
WELL THEN, WE'RE GONNA NEED MORE LIGHT
YOU GOT EXTRA BATTERIES
HERE THEY ARE

THESE
SHOULD
WORK.

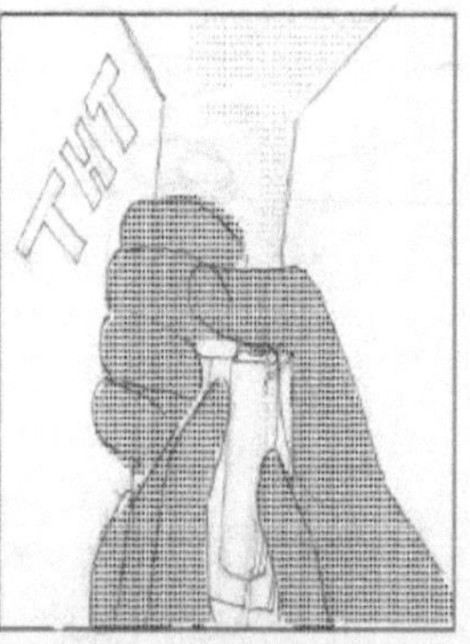

THT

PERFECT.

ALRIGHT
LETS
GO
!!!!

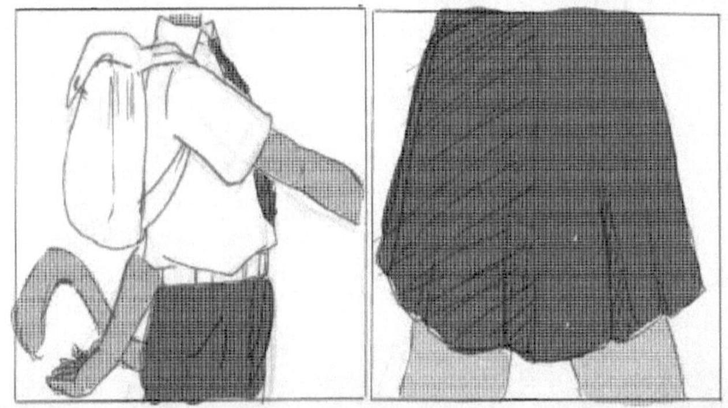

HEY
ITS GETTING BRIGHTER

AND I HEAR MORE WATER.

WOW..

I WONDER HOW DEEP THAT WATER IS
KRSSH!

PEI WHAT ARE YOU DOING !!!

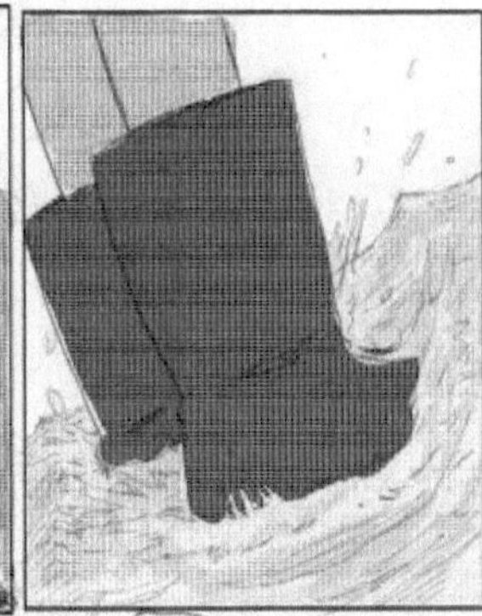

WATER IS FINE,

AND LOOK....

KRSK
THERE ANOTHER CREVEST.

EH

AH
TMP

UN

WAIT
!!!

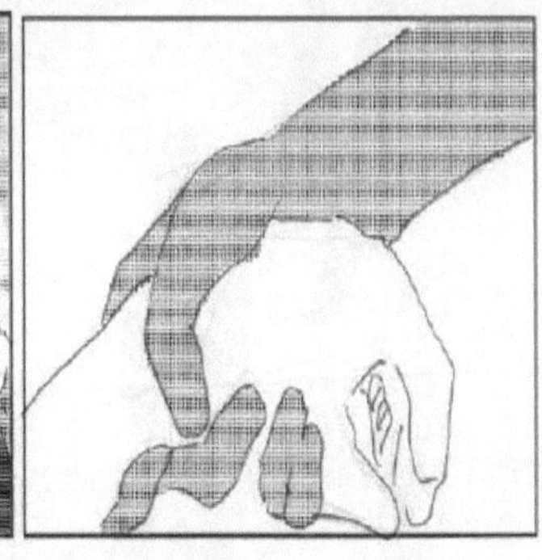

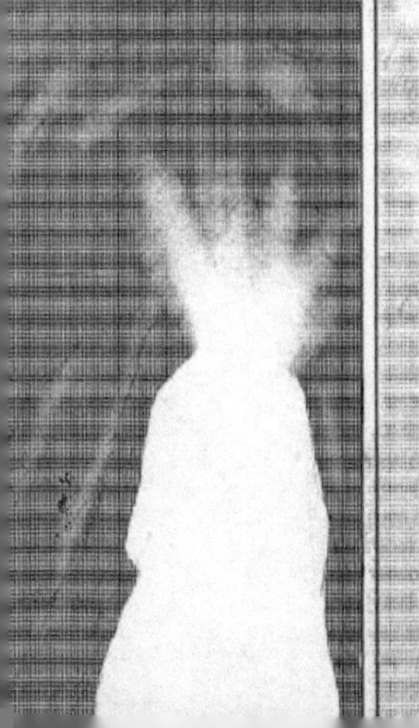

WOAH
I DIDN'T
KNOW
THIS
EXISTED
HERE.

S
S
H
H
H

TRY NOT TO GET HURT PLEASE !!!!
OUT WHAT THAT THING IS.
BUT WE HAVE TO FIND
THING ?
HAS SHE LOST HER MIND.
I DONT SEE A TH-

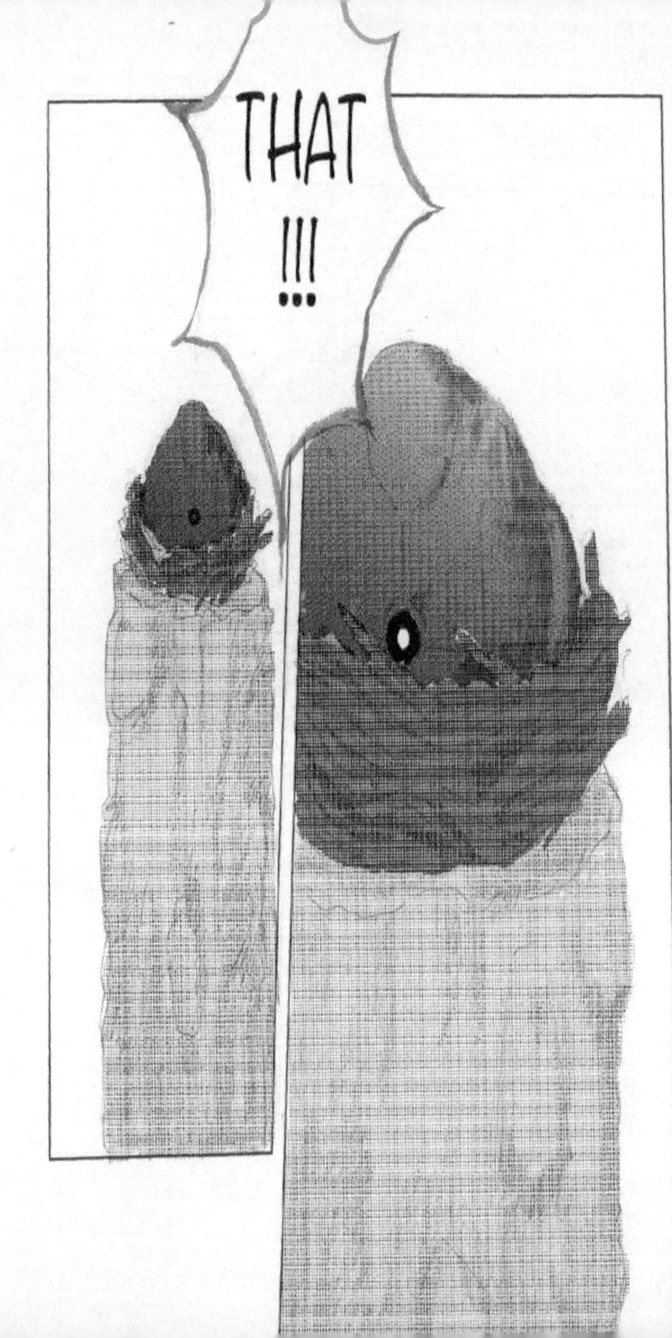

THAT
!!!
...

CHAPTER
DANGER
6
TNT
TNT
TNT
TNT
TNT
TNT
TNT
DON'T TOUCH

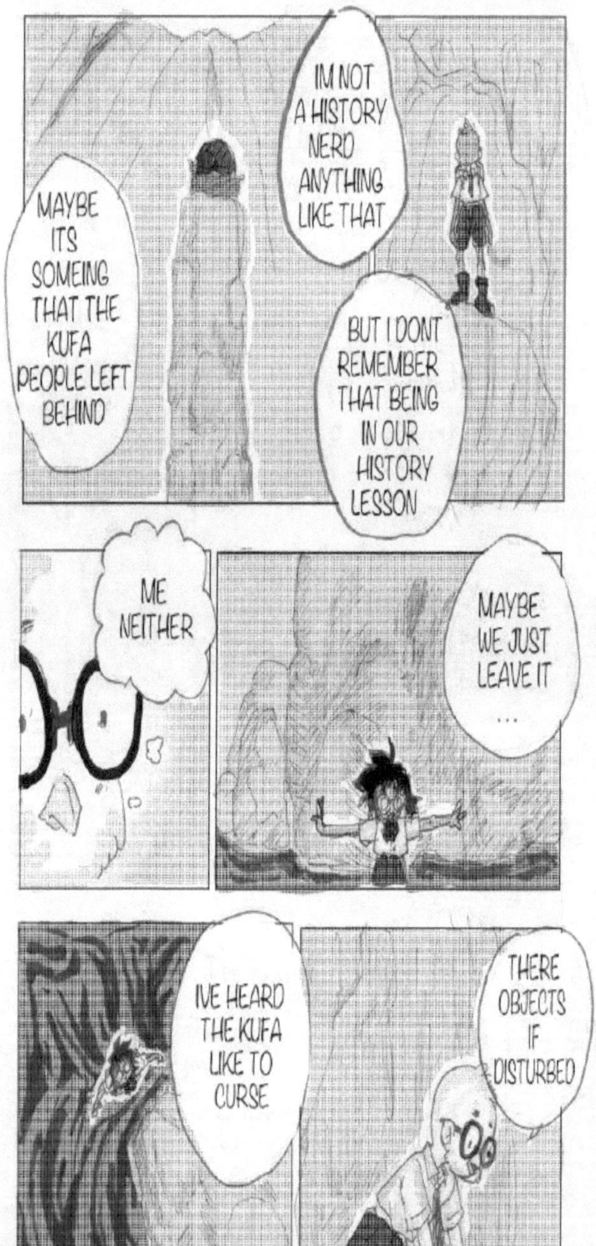

IM NOT A HISTORY NERD ANYTHING LIKE THAT
MAYBE ITS SOMEING THAT THE KUFA PEOPLE LEFT BEHIND
BUT I DONT REMEMBER THAT BEING IN OUR HISTORY LESSON
ME NEITHER
MAYBE WE JUST LEAVE IT ...
IVE HEARD THE KUFA LIKE TO CURSE
THERE OBJECTS IF DISTURBED

AAHH PEI ARE YOU CRAZY? !!!!!!

WELL, WE WON'T KNOW UNTILL WE SEE WHAT IT IS FIRST?

HUFF
HUFF
HUFF
HUFF
HUFF

HUFF
HUFF
HUFF

AWE...

GRAB

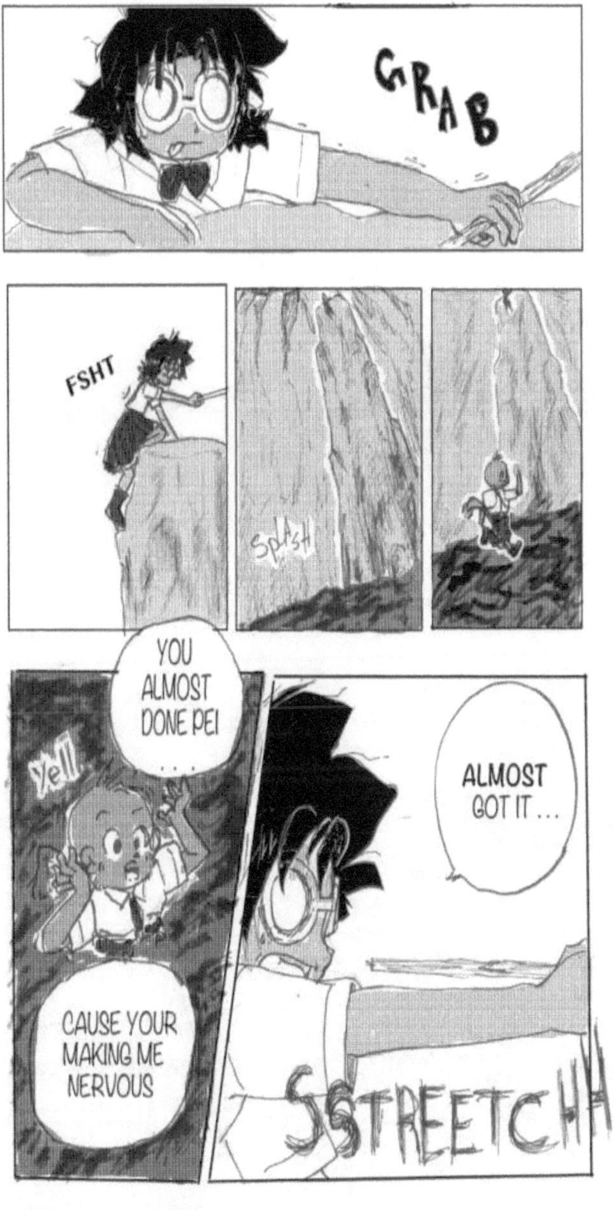

FSHT

Splsh

YOU ALMOST DONE PEI
...
Yell
CAUSE YOUR MAKING ME NERVOUS

ALMOST GOT IT ...
SSTREETCH

POKE
POKE
CLICK
WHAAAHH
AHHHHH
AHHHH
AHHHHH

WOOOOOSH

HN!?
EH?

THUD
SplAH

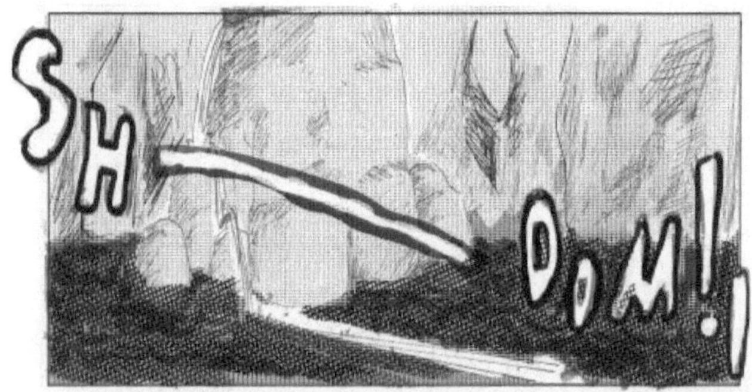

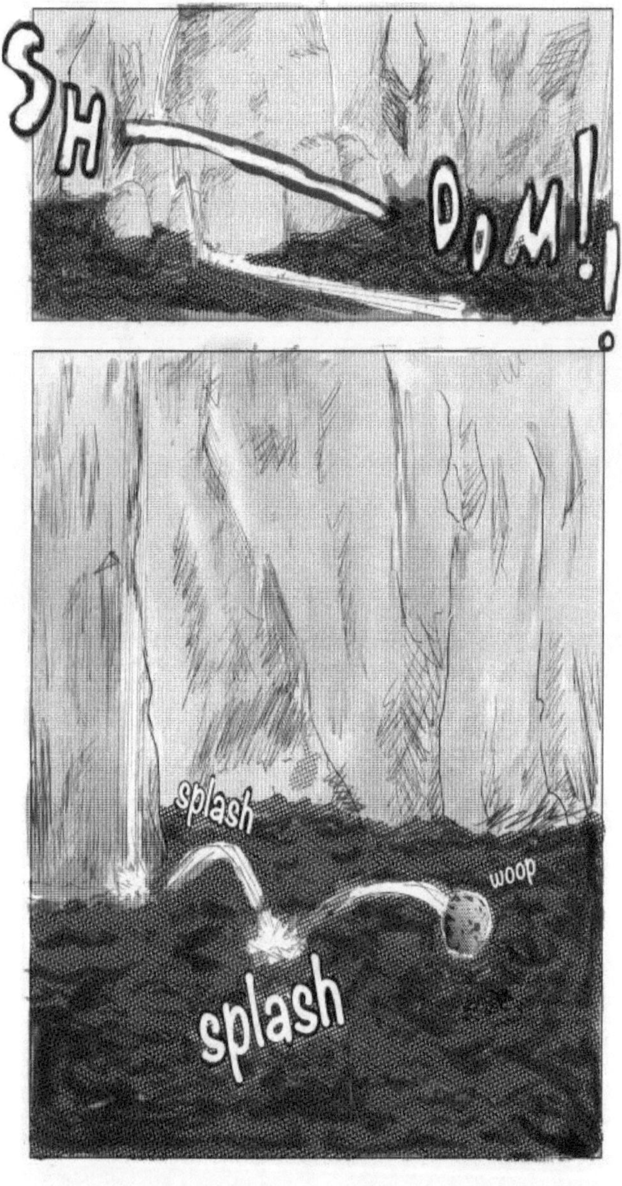

SH
OOM!!

splash
woop
splash

PEI, ARE ...
YOU OK ?

YEA, YOU ?
IM OK.

WHAT HAPP- ENED ...
SHOOOM
DID YOU SLIP 'N FALL. ?.

NO... THE OBJECT, I PRESSED IT ....
THEN THIS FORCE JUST
BLEW ME BACK
AND UH... I DON'T KNOW.

I'M NOT GOING CRAZY
. . .

SEE, LOOK OVER THERE !!!

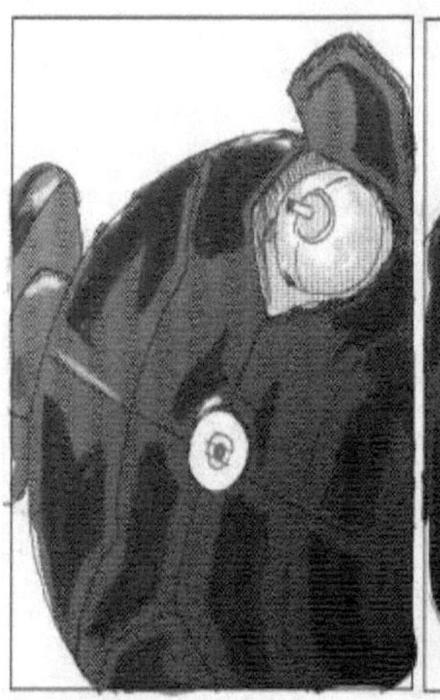

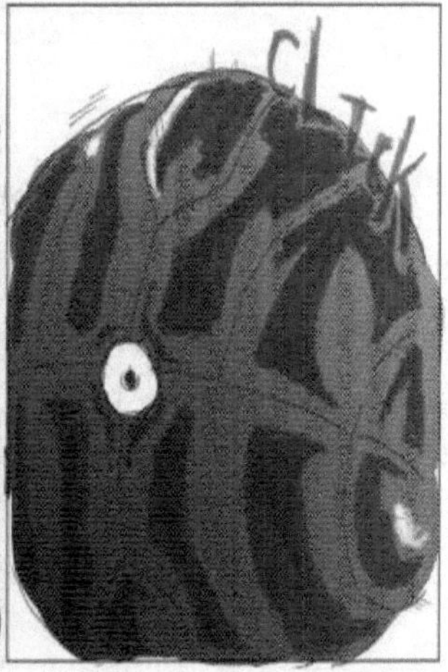

CLICK

• • •

WE
NEED
TO
LEAVE
NOW

UH
!?
Bonk
KRSCHT
!

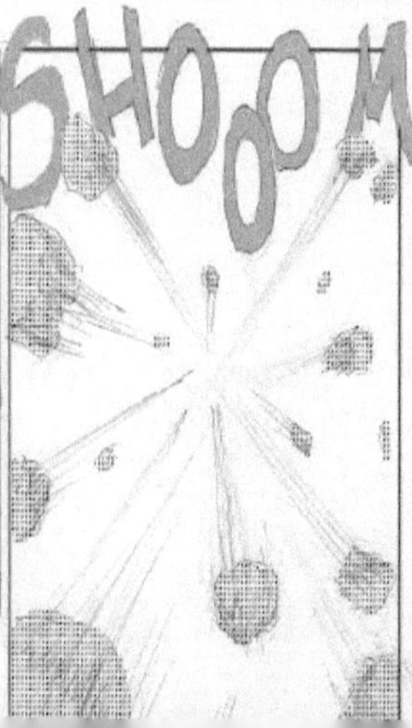
SHOOOM

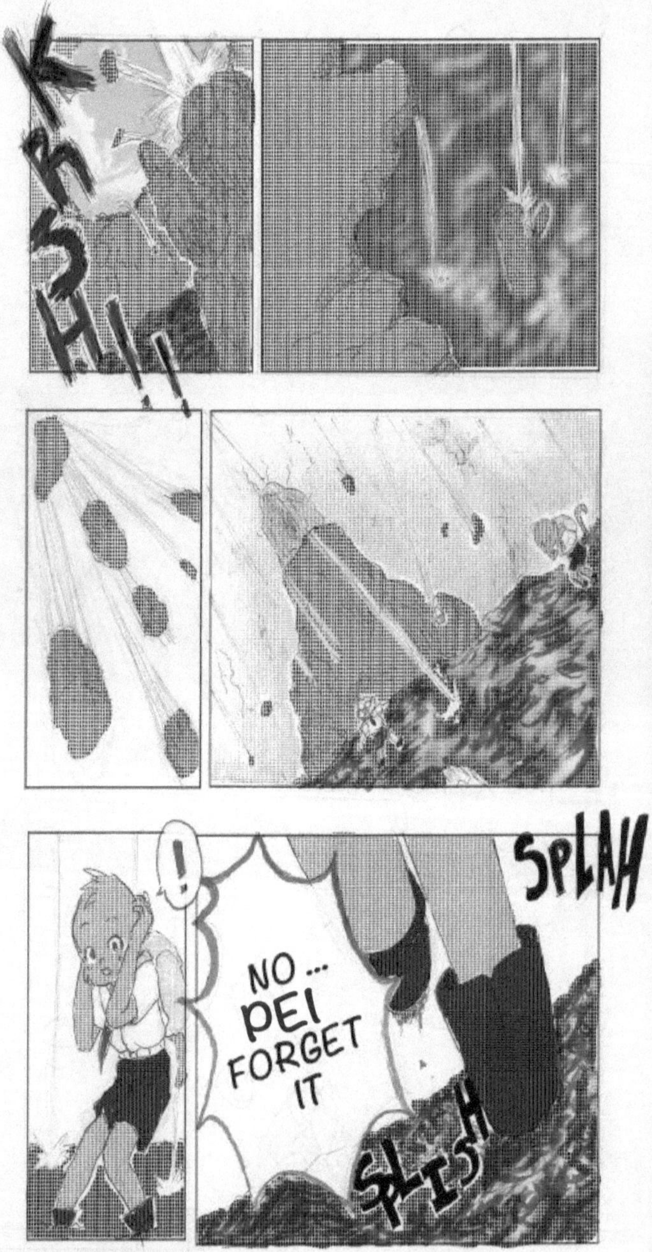

KRSH!!
SPLAH
NO...
PEI
FORGET
IT
SPLISH

phst
HGN
Tmp
GOT
CHA
!!!

phst
phst
phst
KRSK
phst
phst

UNN
RATTLE
RATTLE 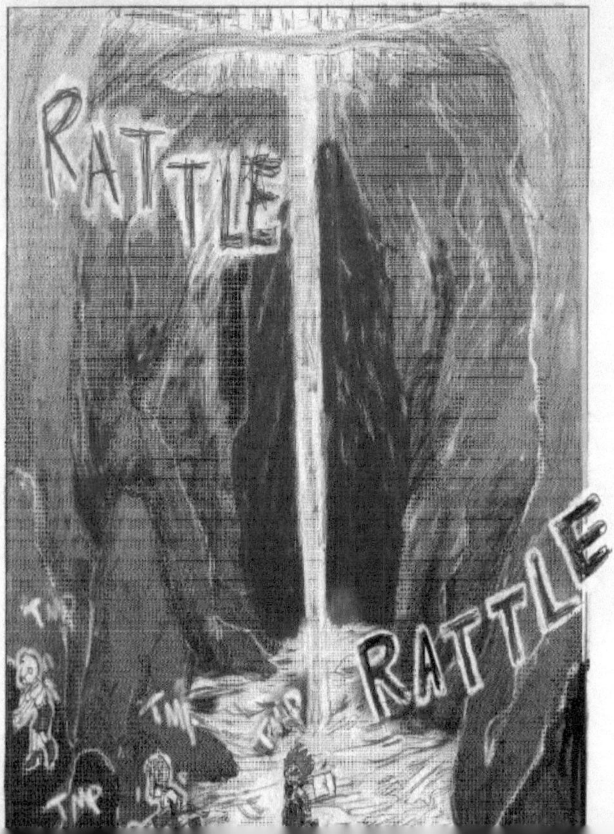

RATTLE
RATTLE

TMP
TMP

TMP
TMP
TMP
TMP

HUFF
HUFF
HUFF
BANG
GA

OUCH
THUD

THERE YOU ARE, WE'RE WONDERING SCARED SOMETHING MIGHT HAVE
...
HAPPENED. BREAKING THE RULES IS FORBIDEN YOU KNOW THAT

YOU THREE TO THE CANTEENA
...
NOW !!!

SEE, I TOLD YOU...
TMP
TMP
TMP

IT WASN'T WORTH IT.
FSH

CANTINA

I CANT BELIEVE YOU ACTUALLY RISKED TO GET THAT THING...
IT WAS PROBABILLY SOMETHING THE KUFA FORGOT ANYWAY.

HEY... I WANT TO SEE IT UP CLOSE.

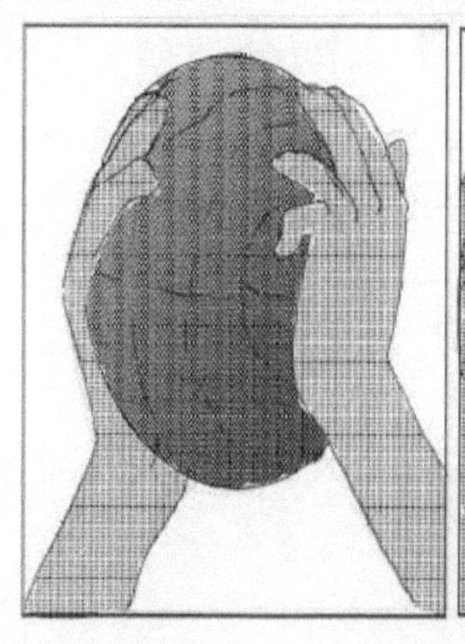

ISN'T SUPOSSED TO DO SOME- THING.

IT LOOKS OLD, HOW MUCH YOU WANNA BET THAT THING IS PROBALY BROKEN? WHAT A WASTE.

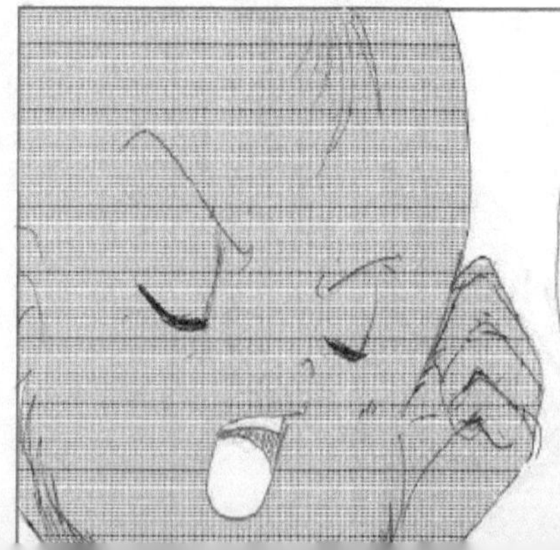

I DON'T KNOW WHY YOU EVEN GOT THAT THING ANYWAY...

CHAPTER

7

SUMMER

BEGINS

ALRIGHT CHILDREN, DO YOU HAVE ANY QUESTIONS WHILE
WE WRAP UP THIS TOUR
SITE 4

NO... OK THEN
FALCUTY, WE THANK YOU FOR THE OPPERTUNITY

FOR ALLOWING US TO GIVE A A PEICE OF HISTORY
AND TO TEACH OUR WORLD
AS TO WHY IT'S TO BE RESPECTED

AND WITH THAT, IT IS BULT TO UNDERSTAND BY THOSE
IN THE PRESENT, CREATED BY THOSE IN PAST

THAT ALL TOGETHER CREATES THE
EVERYDAY, FUTURE BOTH BIG AND SMALL

STUDENTS, I HOPE YOU
ADOPTED WHAT YOU'VE LEARNED AN APPLY IT IN YOUR LIVES.

DUN
DUN

HUMMING
HMM HMHM

!

TMP
TMP

TU
BUM
DEFINTLY NEED MORE IMAGES TO PUT IN THIS PHOTO ALBUM
Growl
LAUGHS I HAVEN'T FORGOT ABOUT YOU TOO !!!
GROWL

BLAH
BLAH
BLAH

NOW CLASS, IM GLAD THAT MOST OF YOU WERE ON YOUR BEST BEHAVIOR.
WHEN WE GET INSIDE WE'LL REVIEW WHAT YOU
...
ALL LEARNED AND WHAT YOUR NEXT YEARS GOALS ARE MIDDLE SCHOOL.

35 MINUTES LATER...
OH GOSH ...
I CANT BELIEVE ITS FINALLY HERE?
YOU'LL BE PRETEENS, AND SOON
VENTRUING OFF INTO YOUR INTEREST

AS TEENS,
TO YOUNG ADULTS.

OH... I PROMISED MYSELF...
I WOULD'T CRY.

I AM TRULY GOING TO MISS YOU ALL.
WILL MISS YOU TOO MISS FRIZZEL !!!!

YOU'D THINK I'D BE USED TO THIS
BY NOW.
ONE MINUTE AND YOU'LL BE OFFIACLY SIXTH GRADERS
YELL
AND SUMMER BEGINS !!!!!
YEA !!!
FIVE
FOUR
THREE
TWO
ONE !!!

UM... MRS. FRIZZLE, IT WAS MY IDEA
....
TO GO TO THE CAVES.

IM REALLY SORRY.
OH DEAR IT WASNT ABOUT
....
ME BEING ANGRY
....
IT WAS ABOUT KEEPING

YOU ALL SAFE.

OF COURSE NOT
YOUR MENTALLY GROWING KIDS
I FULLY EXPECT MISTAKES
IM GLAD YOUR OUR ...
TEACHER MRS. FRIZZLE
SEE YA MRS. FRIZZLE
WE'LL MISS YOU

TMP
TMP
SIGH
MAN, HOW LUCKY ARE
WE TO HAVE A TEACHER
LIKE THAT.

IM JUST GLAD THAT THIS
WAS AT THE END OF THE YEAR.!!!
THX

FSSSTT
HHTT
SHH
SHH
OB
OB
SH
SH
OOOOOOO

MAN, I CAN'T WAIT FOR
I GOT FOR THIS SUMMER
YOU TO SEE THE LIST
uh...yea, ABOUT THAT.. IT WILL HAVE TO WAIT UNTIL LATER PEI
GOTTA GO TO MARTIAL ARTS CAMP TOMORROW.
IT ONLY HAPPENS ONCE IN EVERY FIVE YEARS. !!!!!
BESIDES THE WORLD'S GREATEST TEACHER IS GOING TO BE THERE. I MEAN HOW COOL IS THAT. UH!?
... YEA

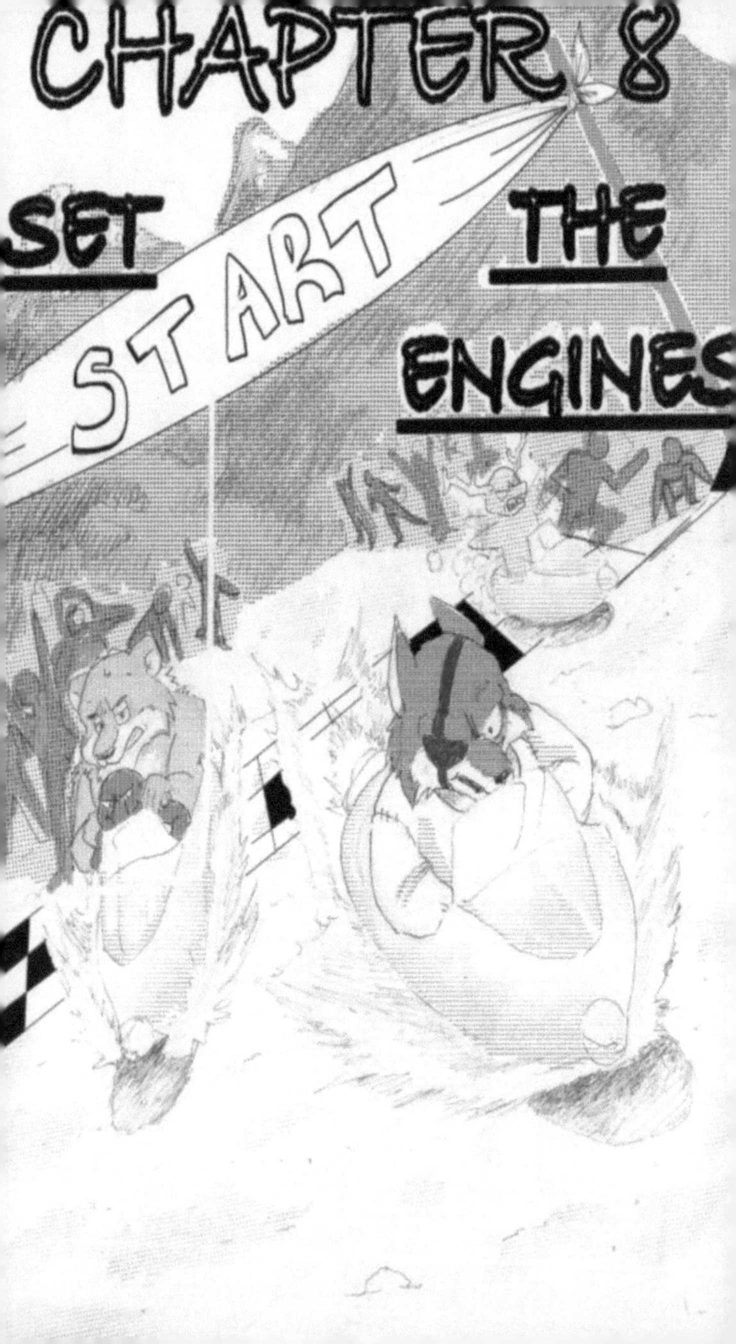

CHAPTER 8

SET THE ENGINES

YOU CAN DROP ME OFF HERE.
THUD

JUMP
THUD

SEE YA IN...
TWO WEEKS GUYS...
BYE.

SHUDOOOSHAAA!!!
HEY, PEI
NOT YOU TOO ....
SORRY ...
IT'LL ONLY BE TWO WEEKS PEI, THEN I'M FREE ALL SUMMER
TO DO WHAT WE WANT.
"SIGH"
OK.

THUD

TSH

SLIDE

TMP

WE'LL BE BACK SOON, THEN WE CAN START OUR SUMMER TOGETHER OK
ALRIGHT
....

THUD

WOOOOO

IT WAS OK.
OK? SO SOMTHING HAPPEND AT SCHOOL TODAY
SO...HOW WAS YOUR SCHOOL TRIP DEAR?

OH DEAR IM SURE WHATEVER IT WAS
IT'LL BE OK IN TIME

SOME-TIMES YOU HAVE
TO FORGET ... FOCUS ON
POSITIVE SIDE AND LET THE NEGATIVE GO.

TRY TO PARTICE MORE MINDFUL-NESS.
NOW COME, LETS GET SOME
SNACKS AND RELAX

BEEP
BEEP
BEEP
BEEP
!

SIR
WE'VE GOT A SIGNAL

WOOOOSH
SCRATCH

IT SEEMS
ITS SOME
FAR OFF
DISTANT
PLANET

ON
A COASTAL
LINE

TMP
TMP

GOOD

WHAT ARE THEIR VALUABLE RESOURCES?
ITS FILLED A LOT OF
METALS AND COALS SIR..
40% COAL AND 60% METAL
HUMPH !!
THE KEY IS MORE IMPORTANT
BUT TAKING THEIR STUFF
DOES SOUND NICE.
GO CHECK THE FUEL TANKS.
ALRIGHT THEN.
LISTEN UP MEN. !!!!

HERE THE PLAN

LITSEN UP
WE'LL BE TAKING A LAP TO THIS PLANET
TO GET THE KEY IN HOPES TO ENSURE
OUR SURVIVAL

THAT IS THE MISSING PEICE TO OUR
OUR FUTRUE
AND ABUN-DANCE

WE'LL USE THE KEY TO STEAL ENDLES
GOODS TO TRADE IN THE MARKET

EH I DONT MEAN TO BE RUDE
OR INTERRUPT OIR.
BUT WHAT ABOUT OUR PLANET?

BLOW IT UP !!!

I WIILL NOT LET MY SURVIVAL REST IN THE HANDS...
OF YOU MORONS.
DO IT NOW,
OR I'LL HAVE YOUR BUTTS
AND HEADS !!!!
SIR... I HAVE TO REPORT THAT THE FUEL TANKS ARE LOW AND
WE WON'T BE MAKING IT EARTH.

HM.

A PLAN B
WILL HAVE
TO BE
THOUGHT
OF

WHY
DON'T WE
JUST USE
THE
ENERGY
OF THE

TO
POWER
OUR SHIP

I
KNOW

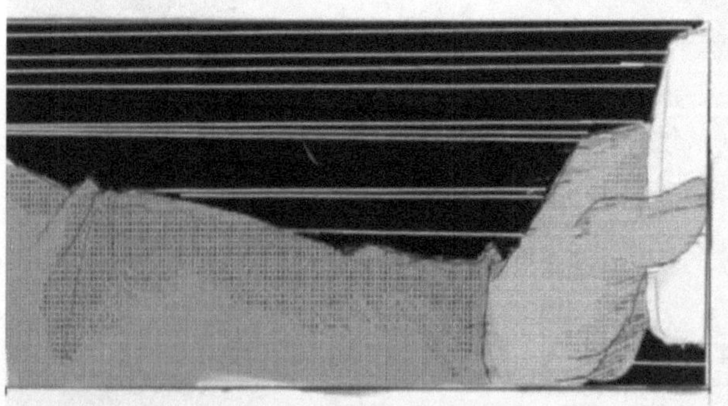

LISTEN UP YOU FOOLS WE GOT A CHANGE OF PLANS.
SINCE WE'RE OUT OF EXTRA FUEL WE'RE GOING TO HAVE TO BE MORE CREATIVE.

INSTEAD COAL TO POWER OUR SHIP, WE'LL JUST USE THE KEY'S ENERGY

SO HERE IT IS... !!!
WE'LL TAKE THE CURRENT
TO CUT DOWN ON TIME.

CYPHEN IT FOR RESOURCES
WE'LL GO TO THIS EARTH,

THEN WE'LL USE THE KEY FOR ENERGY
TO POWER THE SHIP. AND
ONCE I HAVE ACCESS

TO EVERYTHING ....
IT ALL WILL BECOME MINE.

THE ENGINES ARE READY
FOR TAKE OFF WHENEVER READY SIR.

EXCELLENT...

CAUSE THE LAST THING I NEED IS THOSE PSYCOPATHS SHOWING UP AND SPOILING THE PARTY.

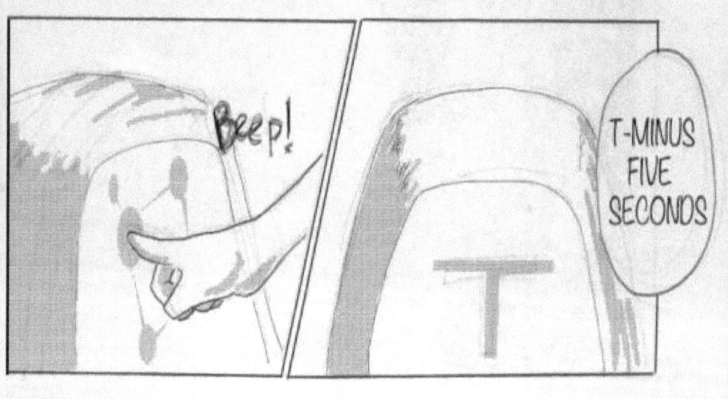
START THE COUNTDOWN
Beep!
T-MINUS FIVE SECONDS
T

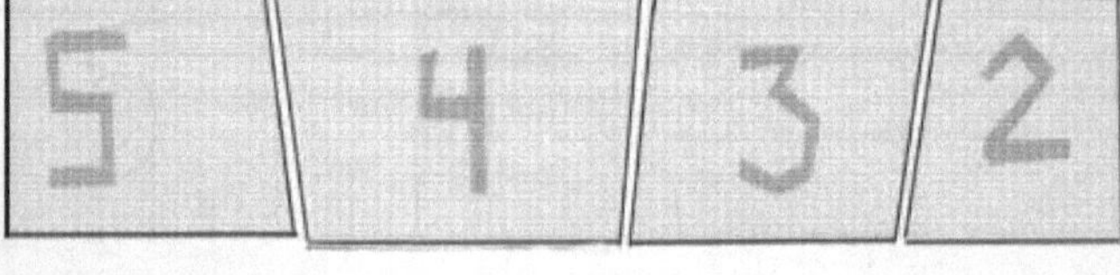
5
4
3
2

FLASH

DAAAX
DAA
BOOOM!
BBOO
ONE
!!!

SHHH
HTTT

NOW....
PUNCH IT
TO HYPER-
SPEED

AND
GET
US THE
HELL OUT
OF HERE
!!!!!!!!
....

CHAPTER 9

GOODBYE FOR NOW

went to
the store
-be right
back....
Clean up
ROOM please.
?

WE'LL
I GUESS
IT...
DOES
NEED
A LITTLE
CLEANING.

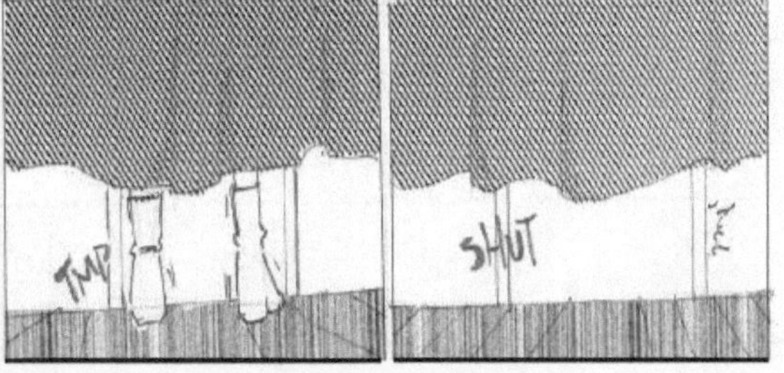

THRIF
ROLL
THUD
ROLL
STOP
BATH-
ROOM
TIME.
TMP
SHUT

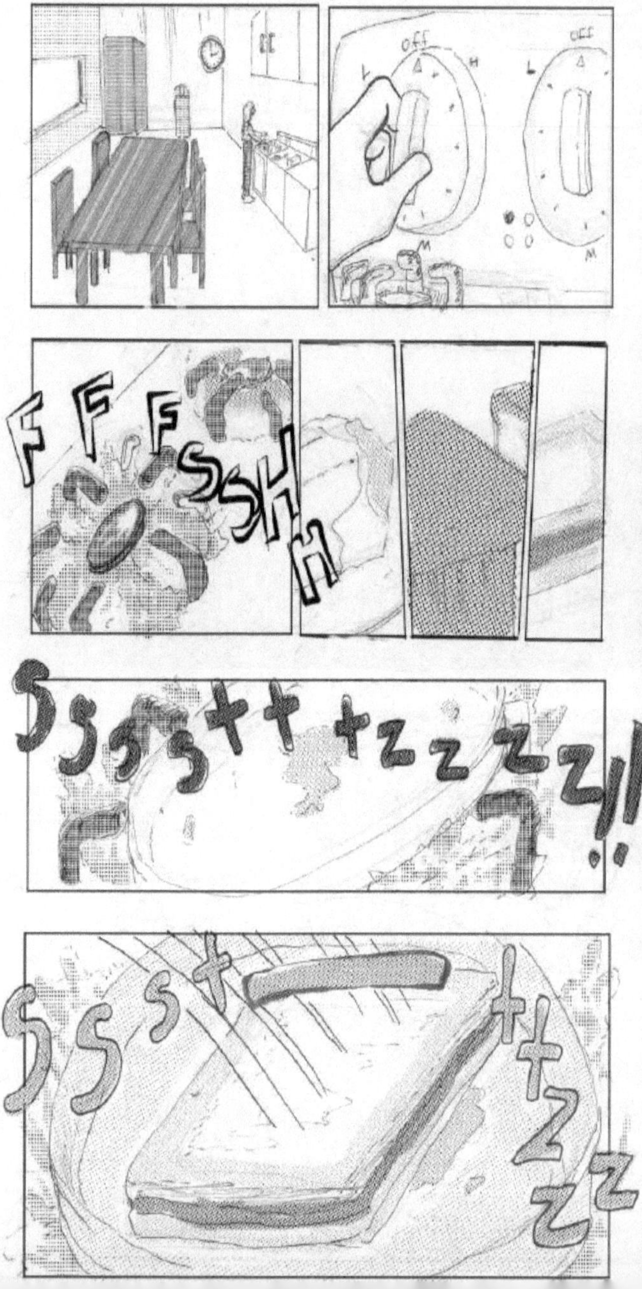

FFF
SSH!
SSStttzzzzz!!

SSStttzzz

FSSH!
BOY I CAN'T WAIT TO GET STARTED
ON MY MARTIAL ARTS CAMP.
OW
TAR
I HOPE PEI'S NOT TOO UPSET...
THIS IS A CHANCE FOR ME TO BE THE GREATEST
AND ONE DAY OPEN MY OWN STUDIO AFTER MY IDOL...
HO-CHEN.
PIN
2ND

LAST SUMMER MISSED.
I JUST COULDN'T PASS THIS TIME.
MMM...
I SHOULD TAKE THESE STONES FOR GOOD LUCK
HUN...ITS SHEN, HE SAID HE'S LEAVING
SOON. AND HE WANTS YOU TO MEET
HIM AT YOUR PICK UP SPOT
SO YOU ALL CAN SAY YOUR GOODBYES,
ALSO ITS CLOSER TO HIS CAMP SITE.
SO ARE YOU READY TO GO THEN?
YEA.
THRF
DEAR, ARE YA SURE YOU DONT NEED A
RIDE ON THE WAY THERE.?
NO MOM

HN!

YOU SURE YOU DON'T
NEED A RIDE?
YOUR GETTING EMBAR-SSING.

?!
UH
MY TIRES... ARE FLAT
WHAT... I JUST FIXED THIS.
WELL... I GUESS YOU NEED THAT RIDE AFTER ALL.

SEE, THIS ISN'T TOO BAD UH?
LOOK I'M NOT A BABY, OK MOM.
AFTER THIS, THATS IT.
OK.

open
DAD, WE NEED TO HURRY!

RELAX SON, YOU STILL GOT TIME LEFT.

I KNOW DAD, BUT THIS WELL BE THE LAST
TIME I GET TO DO THIS SO I DON'T WANT TO MISS IT.

SH O

O O M

I HOPE POW'S BUS DOSENT...
LEAVE BEFORE I GET THERE.

BLAH
BLAH
BLAH
BLAH

V R O O M

IT LOOKS LIKE WE
MADE DECENT TIMING...
BUT GOSH, I WONDER WHERE
THE REST OF BUSES ARE?
ITS 10 TILL ALREADY.
JUST SIT AND WAIT I GUESS..?
OH MY SWEET BOY, FINALLY ON
ON HIS OWN FOR THE
FIRST TIME WITHOUT ME.
MOM...
hm?
TSHOOMA
Ssshh

POW, SHEN... WHERE ARE YOU?
HELLO... EARTH TO GUYS.
HEY YOU FINALLY MADE IT.

BEFORE YOU GO I HAVE SOMETHING FOR YOU.
ODD... I THOUGHT I WAS THE GIFT GIVER.

HERE..
HUH?
WHAT'S THAT?

A WALKIE TALKIE
?
SO I CAN KEEP UP WITH ...
YOU GUYS' CAMP DAYS
OVER THE COURSE OF
THE NEXT TWO WEEKS.
DONT BE SAD PEI,
LOOK.. WHEN WE GET
BACK, I PROMISE WE WILL
DO THINGS ONLY YOU
ENJOY FOR THE REST OF THE SUMMER.

HO
N K

HEY
GUYS
...

DONT SAY
GOODBYE
WITH OUT ME
!!!

SORRY, WE'RE LATE,
WE TOOK THE SHORT CUT
AND GOT STUCK IN TRAFFIC.
YOU'VE SHOULD'VE TAKEN THE HIGH-
ALL STUDENTS NOW REPORT FOR CAMP BUSES.
POW...THE BUSES ARE HERE.
IT'S TIME.
WE'LL I'LL SEE YOU GUYS
IN TWO WEEKS.

IM REALLY GOING TO MISS YOU GUYS...
HUG?
KEEP ME POSTED OK.

SEE YA LATER.
OH YEA.
HERE
UH ... A WALKIE TALKIE.

SO YOU CAN KEEP ME UPDATED
WITH YOUR STUDIES.
HONK
HONK
COME ON SON !!!
TIME IS A TICKING
HAVE A GOOD TIME
DOING YOUR RESEARCH !!!!
SO...
WHAT THE PLAN WITH YOU AND RAJ?
WE'LL

BEEP
BEEP
BEEP
SORRY DEAR BUT GOTTA RUN
ITS JUNE'S DINNER TIME ABOUT NOW
BUT DONT WORRY IM SURE YOU'LL FIND SOMTHING CREATIVE.

MAYBE.. SAY HI TO JUNE FOR ME.

RumblE
Rumble

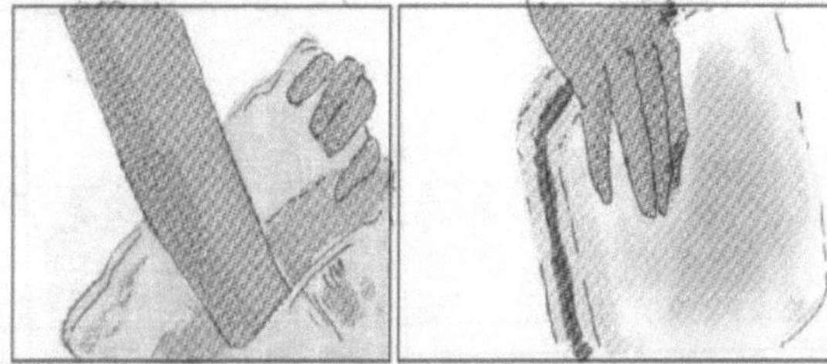

CHOP

CHAPTER 10

WHATS MY PURPOSE?

SSHHINH
TMP
TMP
CHWIGGLE
FLICK
TMP
TMP

WOW...
LOOK AT
THAT
WATER
GO...
THUD

RuM
ble

IS THAT YOUR STOMACH OR MINE.
!
LUCKLY FOR US ...
PAT PAT
TiF TiF
I GOT JUST ANOTHER SNACK.
TA-DA !!!

RIP

I WISH I HAD A TALENT OR SOMETHING COOL ...
TO LOOK FORWARD TOO.
SOB
HMM
SNIF
SNIF

HM...I DON'T EVEN KNOW WERE TO START.
IM NOT GOOD AT ANYTHING.

"SIGH" MAYBE THEY'RE RIGHT...
I'LL BE FORGOTTEN AND A NOBODY ...
NO, I I'M GOING FIND MY PURPOSE ...

EVEN IF IT KILLS ME. !!!!!

LOOK.. IT'S..
THE TEMPLE.

HM....
MAY IT
BEGIN.

AH...THE FRESH PUPILS. HAVE ARRIVED.
YOU ARE HERE TO GAIN AND LEARN, CADETS.
LISTEN UP, THIS ISNT A VACATION
BUT FIRST WE'LL BE SEEING HOW YOU FAIR BEFORE CRACKING LIKE THE "SOFT EGGS" THAT YOU ALL ARE.

IT FEELS LIKE SUCH A DREAM...
I'M REALLY HERE, AREN'T I....
YOUR ON YOUR OWN NOW CADETS....
GOODLUCK.
YOU'LL NEED IT.

TMP
TMP
TMP
TMP
SHUT
ITS REALLY HIM...
HO-CHEN
. . .
HMPH...

NOW...
LET THE TRUE GROWTH BEGIN.
VRRRRNNN

VROOM!
NNRRRNN
WOW.. WERE
GOING SO FAST DAD

AND I CAN EVEN SEE THE TOP OF THE MOUNTAINS FROM HERE.

HEY, DO YOU THINK THEY'LL STILL
REMEMBER ME.?
SHOOM
CAUSE ITS BEEN A WHILE SINCE I
LAST SAW THEM.

HEY ITS CLYDE
AND MADE GOOD TIMING AT THAT.
!?
Open
AND GUESS WHO ELSE HERE...

MR. WISS...
HEY THERE KIDDO...
!?
GLAD YOU CONVICED YOUR PA FOR YOU TO COME,

BECAUSE WE GOT CHA A PRESENT YOU'LL LIKE...
HUFF
HUFF
WOW, COOL
HUFF
HUFF

HUFF
HUFF
HUFF
WE PROMISE YA.

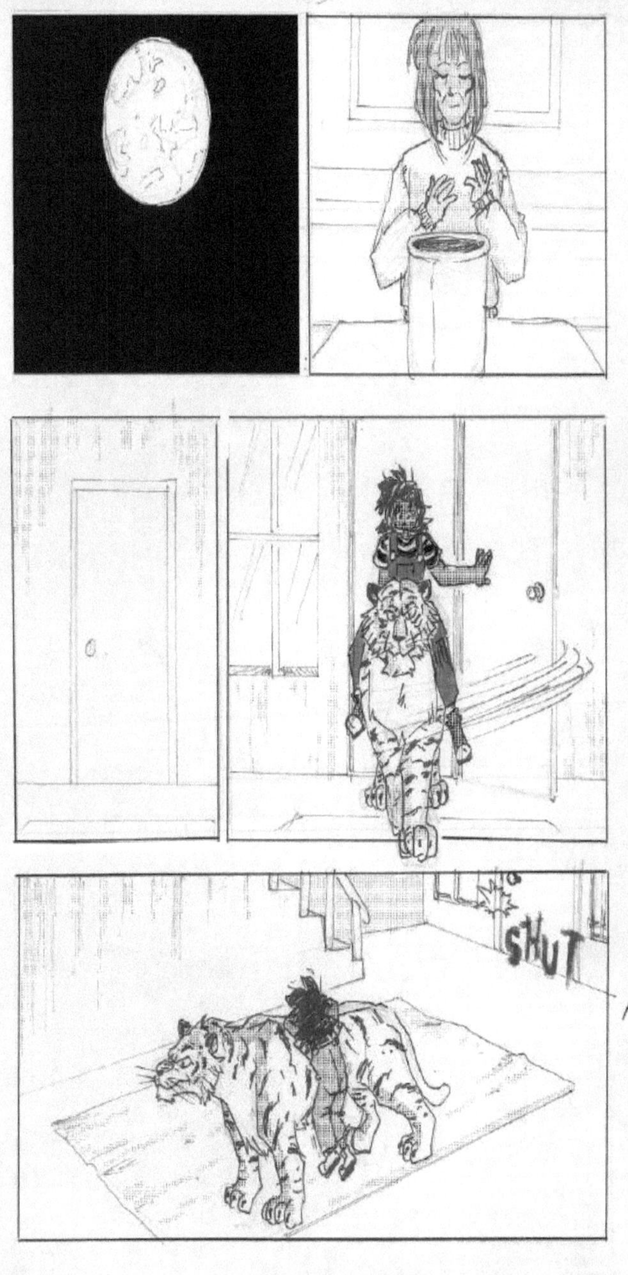

SHUT

MAN, THAT SMELLS GOOD
WHAT FOR DINNER?

FRIED SHRIMP AND POTATOES.

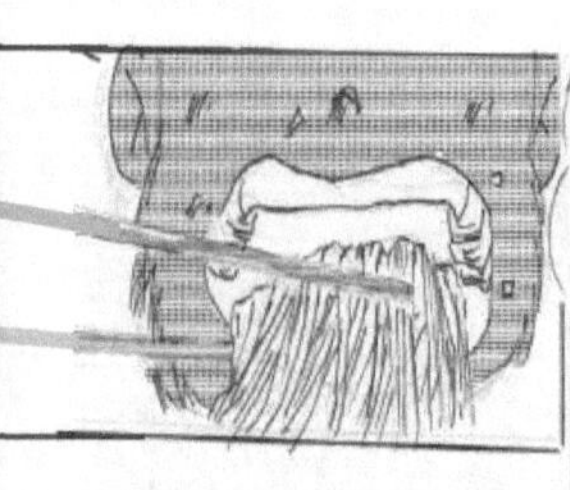

I GOTTA SCALF AR. THIS DOWN AND
GET READY FOR THE TEST THIS WEEK.
TiiF
Tils

SL URi

BOY THESE STEAKS SURE LOOK GOOD.
HEY SON, COME AND GET SOME BEFORE WE EAT THEM ALL.
FWSH

TMP
TMP
FSH

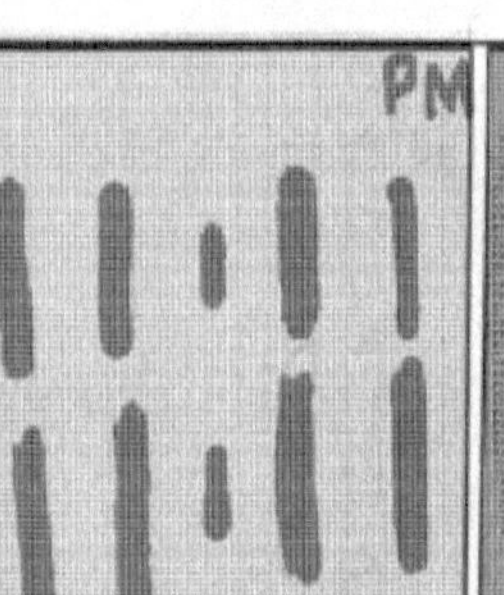

PM
11:11

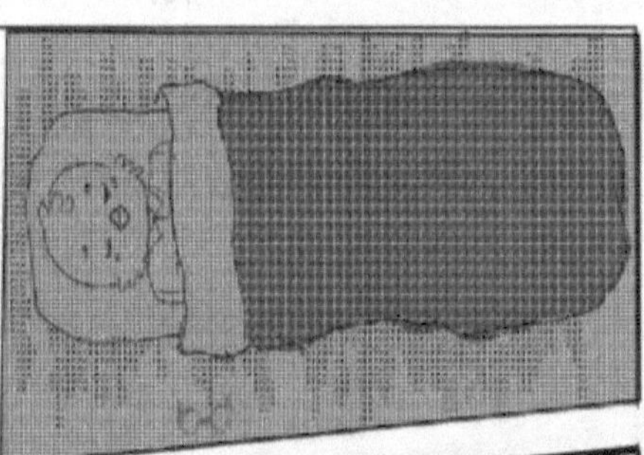

FSH

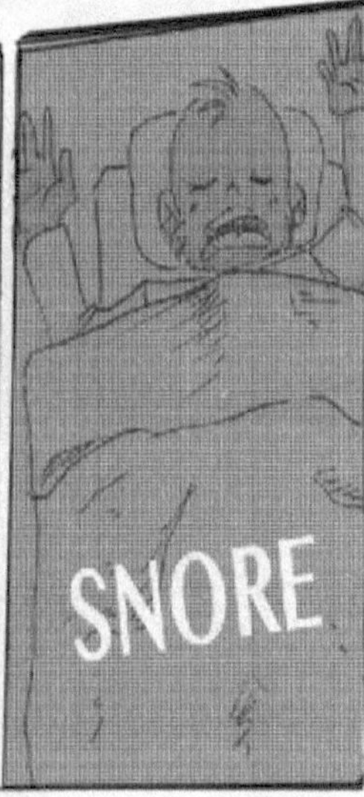

SNORE

KEY FACTS...

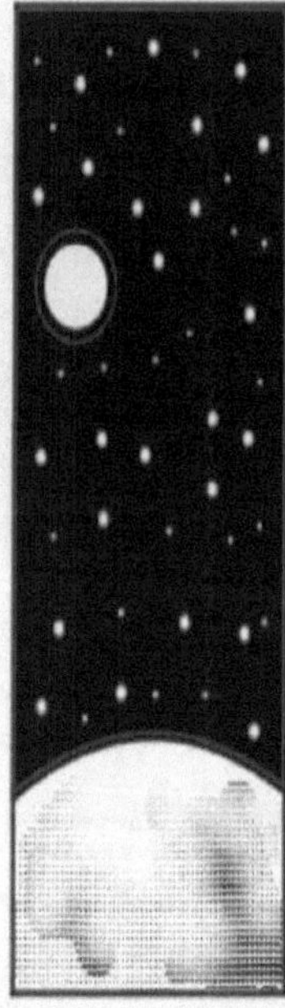

ENVIROMENT

CHARACTERS

MYSTERY PAGE

LOCATION: EARTH

CITY: TOWNS CITY
STATE: BALDIMIR

ENVIROMENT

THE KUFA

-KUFA PEOPLE MUTATING ONCE MORE BY A MUSHROOM VARIENT.

-THUS CREATING TOWNS AND CITIES USING UNIVERSIAL GEOMERTY.

WHISPERING MOUNTAINS

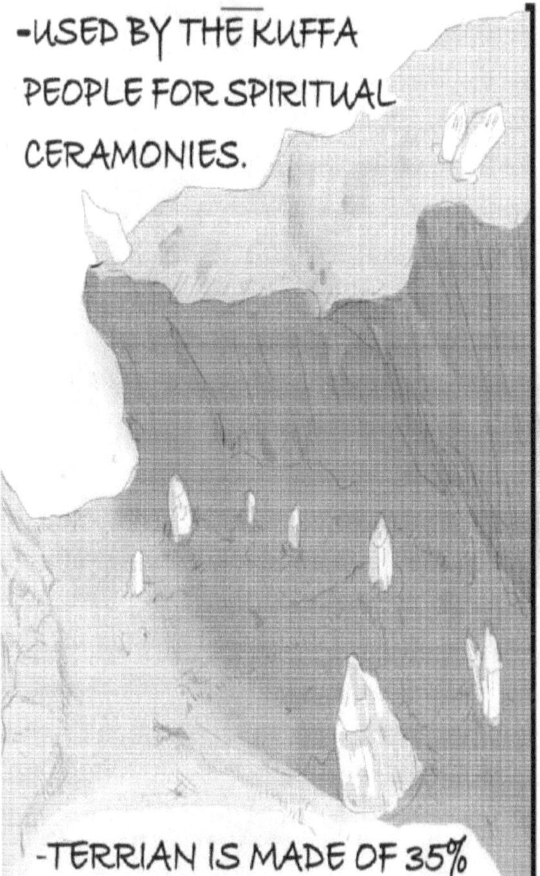

-USED BY THE KUFFA
PEOPLE FOR SPIRITUAL
CERAMONIES.

-TERRIAN IS MADE OF 35%
CRYSTALS, THUS ALLOWS
AN ECHO EFFECT TOWARDS
SOUND.

KEY CHARCTERS

HEIGHT: 3'7"

WEIGHT: 70 lbs

POW DAHN

EXTROVERTED, ACTION ORIENTED, LOYAL, SUPERSTIOUS, COURAGEOUS, ARROGANT, FOOLISH.

KEY CHARCTERS   MARYON HILLS

HEIGHT: "3'5"

WEIGHT: 5 lbs

PERSONALITY

EGOTISTICAL, INSECURE, RESPONSABLE, MATURE, TALKATIVE.

LET THE MATRIX END AND YOUR SOUL BEGIN

YOU ARE
DEALING WITH
COPYRIGHTED WORK,
ANY ATTEMPT
OF INFRINGEMENTS
LEAGALACTION WILL
BE TAKEN.